THE PROVIDER

JOHN DEACON

Copyright © 2024 by John Deacon

All rights reserved.

No part of this book may be reproduced in any form or by any electronic or mechanical means, including information storage and retrieval systems, without written permission from the author, except for the use of brief quotations in a book review.

The Provider is a work of fiction. Characters, names, places, and events are either the product of the author's imagination or used fictitiously. Any similarity to real persons, living or dead, is purely coincidental.

Cover design by Angie on Fiverr

Edited by Karen Bennett

Special thanks to advance readers Chris Gibson, Jeff Benham, Max Thompson, and Cindy Koda.

Want to know when my next book is released? SIGN UP HERE.

❦ Created with Vellum

PROLOGUE

"Her." The white-haired man in the black suit pointed from his carriage to the beautiful young redhead who'd just emerged from the mercantile.

The burly man standing beside the carriage frowned. "That's a problem, Mr. Pew. That's Maggie Dunne."

Pew scowled at his henchman. "And soon she'll be Maggie Pew. Go get her."

"With all due respect, sir, she's more trouble than she's worth."

The old man's eyes stared greedily at the young woman's flaming red hair and shapely form. "She looks like she's worth an awful lot of trouble to me."

"Her daddy wore the blue."

"What? The traitorous scum."

"If you pick her, sir, you're gonna have the bluebellies after you."

Isaac Pew growled with frustration. "All right, all right."

Then the shop door opened, and a smiling brunette emerged and joined the redhead. She wasn't as beautiful or bosomy as the Dunne girl, but she was still a lovely young thing and looked healthy and full of life and laughter.

Ensconced grimly within the gloom of his black carriage, Isaac Pew pointed a crooked finger at the new girl's smiling face. "That one, then."

CHAPTER 1

Will Bentley was a tall, narrow-hipped man with powerful shoulders and big hands. The twenty-four-year-old's square-jawed face was rugged, like a thing hewn of granite, not so much handsome as strong.

He radiated confidence as he turned the heavy rock in his hands, nipping at it with the hammer, shaping it to his will.

"You're from Texas?" Bobby asked, sounding impressed from a few feet away.

Will nodded and dropped his hammer and placed the stone and stepped back to study the wall he was building. It looked good.

All he had to do was cap it. Then he could help the other stonemasons finish their work, and it would be on to the next job, a two-hundred-foot-long, four-foot-high retaining wall surrounding the mansion of a silver baron.

"Were you a rebel, then?" the young laborer asked with awe.

Will looked at him. One of the things Will liked about the Western frontier was how few questions people asked.

But Bobby was only eleven or twelve, just a boy.

"Yes, I wore the gray. Most everybody back home did. Not Mr. Dunne, though."

"Who's that?"

"He was my neighbor. He owned a nice ranch beside our small farm."

"And he fought for the Union?"

"That's right."

The boy seemed to think about that for a moment. "Did you fight him?"

Will grinned, thinking this boy clearly did not understand the scope of the war. "No. I never fought Mr. Dunne."

"You hated him, though?"

Will chuckled. "No. I didn't hate him."

The boy looked puzzled. "Why not?"

"He was a good neighbor. His wife and my mama, they study the Bible together every morning. And his daughter, Maggie, is best friends with my little sister."

"But he wore the blue."

"Yes, he did." *And he died wearing it,* Will thought sadly. The war had taken an awful lot of good men on both sides. "Mr. Dunne sided with Sam Houston."

"Who?"

"A good man, a true Texan. He believed in the Union and didn't want to secede. He was afraid secession would destroy Texas."

"Did it?"

"It certainly didn't do it much good. The economy is in shambles. Nobody has any money. Folks are hungry and losing their homes left and right. Which is why I'm here in Denver City."

The boy nodded, seeming to understand. "So you can make money."

"That's right."

"And send it home."

"Yes."

"Oh, so that's why." The boy looked Will up and down, started to say something, and seemed to think better of it.

"That's why what?"

"Nothing."

"That's why I wear these old boots and worn-out homespun clothes?"

The boy nodded sheepishly.

Truth be told, Will was more than a little embarrassed by his tattered clothing. But clothing, even new homespun, cost money, and he was determined to save every penny he could for Mama and Rose.

In a flash, Will pictured his father lying on the ground, covered in blood, already slipping away, and for just a moment, Will was nine years old again, nine years old and scared out of his mind but doing his best not to cry.

You promise, boy?

Nine-year-old Will nodded.

His father snarled then, growling at the pain, and gripped Will's tiny hand all the harder.

Say it, son. I gotta hear you say it.

I promise, Pa. I promise I'll take care of Mama and Rose.

Pa's eyes locked on his then, filled once more with strength and something else, something he would only later realize was pride.

That's my boy. You're the man of the house now.

Will nodded, holding back tears with all his might.

His father groaned again then spoke his final words.

You're the provider.

"I didn't mean no offense," Bobby said, hauling Will back to the present.

"Huh?"

"What I said. Or what I was fixing to say. About the clothes. I didn't mean no offense."

Will shook his head. "None taken. I'd best get back to work."

"All right," Bobby said. But then, in the manner of boys everywhere, he asked another question. "Did you own slaves?"

Will shook his head. "We just had a little pig farm. No slaves. None of the men I fought beside did, either. Maybe the officers. But none of us enlisted men."

"Why fight, then?"

"Because Texas joined the Confederacy. I was loyal to the Republic, not the Union." Will grinned. "Besides, us Texans don't like folks telling us what to do. Especially outsiders."

The boy nodded then looked at Will again, seemingly impressed. "I never knew you was a rebel."

"It's not something I tell many folks," Will said, "and I'd appreciate you not mentioning it to anyone. Otherwise, some Colorado militiaman might start asking me about Glorieta Pass."

"I won't say nothing to nobody," the boy said with solemnity that Will believed. After all, he knew very well how seriously a young man could take a promise.

So seriously that it could set the course of his whole life.

"Well, you'd best go mix some more mud," Will told Bobby. "I'm fixing to top out this wall."

The boy left, and Will turned his attention to a heavy, boxlike stone that would work well as an endcap.

He lifted the rock and studied its angles and composition. Looking for weak points and finding none that mattered, he balanced the big stone on his thigh and started chipping with his rock hammer, flaking away knobs and ridges, shaping the thing patiently, exerting his will against its hard surface.

"Mr. Bentley?" a voice asked.

Will turned to see a boy not much older than Bobby standing there with a piece of paper in his hand and a businesslike expression on his young face.

"That's right. I'm Will Bentley. What can I do for you?"

"Telegram for you, sir."

Feeling a twitch of unease, Will held out his hand. The boy gave him the telegram.

Will read the note in silence, then read it again. And again.

For a moment, Will stood there, his eyes locked on the last line of the telegram.

Life had been good here. Quiet. He'd put his past behind him.

But they said you couldn't escape your past.

And maybe they were right.

Will crumpled the note in his calloused hand and let it drop to the ground. Saying nothing to his fellow stonemasons, he picked up his hammer and walked off the job.

"Where you going, Will?" Bobby called after him.

Will marched away, the hammer swinging at his side.

One of the men picked up the telegram. It was from Will's mother in Clarksville, Texas.

Will Bentley, Denver City, CO – Come home son (stop) We need you (stop) Your sister has been kidnapped (stop)

CHAPTER 2

Eighteen-year-old Rose Bentley paced and prayed.

For weeks, that was all she'd been able to do, pace the wide-plank floors of this well-appointed cottage and beg God to deliver her from this nightmare.

Every time she prayed, she pictured her brother coming for her. But of course, he was a world away in Colorado.

Please, Lord, she prayed, picturing Will, *please save me.*

It had to be soon. She was running out of time.

Pausing at the window, she looked out at the lush, manicured lawns surrounding the estate of the despicable Isaac Pew.

The doctor's carriage was parked in front of the mansion again. She had seen the doctor arrive this morning and carry his little black bag inside.

The doctor looked very similar to Pew himself. Perhaps they were twins. Both men were lean and slightly stooped and favored black suits and flat-brimmed black hats from which flowed ghostly curtains of long, white hair.

If only the doctor were here for Pew and not his wife.

The doctor had been inside for a long time, which frightened Rose.

She set to pacing again. Pacing and praying.

Please don't let her die, Lord. Not yet. Not until Will comes.

Because she knew Will would come for her. Even though she hadn't seen him for years, even though he was nearly a thousand miles away, she knew her big brother would come for her.

She just hoped he got here in time.

For the hundredth time, she tried the door. Locked, of course.

Just beyond the door, she knew, would be one of the guards, one of the rough men who escorted her to the privy and brought her food and drink when she requested it.

"Need something?" a gravelly voice outside the door asked, having apparently heard her touch the handle.

It was Sheffield, the scariest of the guards, a hulking man with an iron grip and eyes that burned like brands in the fire. He always hurried when he took her back and forth, always gripped her arm like a beartrap.

"Yes, I need to go home."

"You are home," he said.

She shuddered at the thought. She couldn't live here. Wouldn't. She would sooner be dead.

She started pacing again.

A few minutes later, a light rapping sounded at the door, chilling her blood.

She stopped pacing and froze there, listening hard, barely breathing.

"Miss Bentley?" Isaac Pew called softly through the door.

Rose said nothing.

"Miss Bentley, I am sorry to have kept you waiting." She heard the old man's breath catch with excitement. "But your wait is almost over. My beloved wife has finally passed away."

CHAPTER 3

The attack came without warning.

Before the gun bellowed from the roadside brush, Will had been lost in thought, wrestling with the same questions that had hounded him over weeks of grueling travel.

Who had taken Rose? Why? Where was she now? Was she okay?

He'd been wondering about these things for weeks, ever since leaving Denver City, riding mile after mile after mile, dawn to dusk, switching mules to help them last.

But now, with only a few more miles to home, someone had taken a shot at him.

Will dismounted, putting himself on the other side of the mule from the shooter, and hauled his .56 Spencer carbine from its boot.

As the unseen attacker fired again, Will dropped to a prone position with his rifle at the ready, scanning the brush.

His mules trotted off, spooked by the attack but too tired to run. And that was good. Because he needed those mules and had a year's wages in a secret compartment at the bottom of one saddle bag.

There was movement in the brush further down the road, but before Will could pay it any real attention, the shooter in the brush fired again.

This time, Will spotted the muzzle flash back in the piney gloom. He stared hard and made out the shape of a man and put his sights at its center and pulled the trigger.

The bandit cried and crumpled into the brush, and then a skinny man dressed in rags burst onto the road and rushed toward the mules.

He was fifty yards away, maybe sixty.

"You touch those mules, you die," Will warned him, but the man had apparently committed to his plan of action because he grabbed the dun mule and mounted from the right side with a desperate leap that made the mule kick and spin, jerking the man around so that Will had just enough time to see his gaunt, terrified face before he fired again and knocked the thief from the saddle.

And just like that, it was over.

No more shots. No more movement. No more bandits.

For the first time in two years, Will had killed men, a thing he'd never expected to have to do again.

It didn't bother him. They had tried to kill and rob him.

It just surprised him was all. Surprised him and sobered him.

He watched the brush across the road for a time. The mules cropped grass another fifty yards down the road. They weren't going anywhere. Not without him. They were plum tuckered out just like he was.

He finally rose up and crossed the road, ready to fire again but not particularly concerned. This might have been his first combat in some time, but four years of war had acclimated his mind to such situations, and he sensed that his enemies were dead or disabled. There had been no further action, no more hollering, no cracking of brush, nothing.

He approached the man in the brush from an angle, just in case. Seeing the man's posture and open eyes, however, he understood this scoundrel had ambushed his last traveler.

As he drew closer, he was surprised by the man's ragged attire and emaciated features—then surprised all over again when he realized that he knew the man.

Not by name. But he knew him, all right. They'd fought together when the 5th Texas Mounted Rifles had joined up with the Magruder's forces in Galveston.

In a flash, he remembered the man carrying cotton bales onto the steamboats, helping to convert the ships into gunboats; remembered him laughing and telling funny stories about picking cotton—a job Will knew all too well—and later still, fighting alongside Will and the other "horse marines" as they recaptured Galveston from the bluebellies.

What had happened to this man?

Why was he so starved down? What had turned him from a valiant, good-natured soldier into a black-hearted, murderous highwayman?

How bad had things gotten here?

He'd seen the signs of trouble as soon as he'd crossed into Texas.

Twice since then, he'd ridden off the road to let bluebellies pass, watching them from cover.

One group went on by, a bunch of soldiers that looked and marched like the closest they'd ever come to battle was drill and ceremony.

The other time, it'd been a cavalry unit, and those boys looked like they had some bark on them.

Sheridan had sent 50,000 Yankee troops to occupy Texas. Will had heard stories of them giving former Confederates a hard time, confiscating weapons and property and baiting men into conflict, then beating them and tossing them into jail, even hanging them on occasion.

Which was unfortunate but not all that surprising.

But he hadn't expected a Texan to try and kill him. For what? The man hadn't known he was carrying money. No one had any money here.

So why kill him?

For a couple of mules and whatever he had in the packs, Will supposed.

That was desperation.

And if these men were that desperate, others would be, too.

Will couldn't afford distractions. He was home again, and home was suddenly as dangerous as the war he'd left behind.

He took the man's Colt Dragoon and ammo pouch and searched him, finding nothing but a hunting knife and a deck of well-worn playing cards.

Suddenly, he remembered the man talking about gambling, bragging about his prowess and luck, saying he had a deck of cards on him if anyone from the 5th wanted to play.

Will couldn't help but wonder if these were the same cards.

"Whatever the case," he told the man, who stared up at him with empty eyes, "your luck's run out."

He considered taking the cards but decided to leave them, figuring there couldn't be any luck left in them, either, then went on down the road and talked to his mules and took a look at the other bandit, who was in even worse shape, as hard as that was to believe, than the ex-soldier.

Barefoot and starved to bone and gristle, the would-be mule thief possessed nothing but the raggedy clothes enshrouding his cadaver.

What a shame. What a senseless shame.

He would have given the men food—money, even—if they'd only asked.

Then he dragged the man off the road and into the brush and gathered his mules and started for home again.

The farm was only a few miles away.

He shook his head.

What a homecoming.

CHAPTER 4

Despite everything—the ambush, his fatigue, the current condition of East Texas, and his concern for Rose—Will felt a surge of excitement as he neared the long path to the farmhouse where he'd been born and raised.

But as he drew closer, he saw the sign.

He reined to a stop and read the unfamiliar green-and-gold sign which stood beside the entrance of the property.

Southern Repose, gilded letters etched into the pine-green sign read.

Will was puzzled.

Southern Repose?

They had never had a sign out front before. What would be the purpose? Everyone around here knew this was the Bentley place.

Not the Southern Repose...

He felt the slightest chill, as if a cloud high in the sky had blocked the afternoon sun.

What was going on here? What was the Southern Repose? And who had put this sign here?

Certainly not Mama. She had never needed a sign before, and she certainly wouldn't go spending the money on one during these hard times.

Rose?

She was a dreamer, a girl who might cook up a ridiculous name like Southern Repose, but where would she get the sign?

He looked up and saw an unfamiliar man come out of the farmhouse carrying a rifle.

Now, who was that?

Will shouldn't have come straight here. And he shouldn't have sat here in plain sight for all the world to see while he was scratching his head over the sign.

Normally, he was a cautious man, a man who liked to size things up before taking action.

Apparently, today was his day for making mistakes. Maybe it was the long trip. Or maybe it was just coming home after all this time.

The man marched toward him, holding the rifle at port arms across his body.

Who was he?

A stranger. A gray-haired stranger with a limp and a paunch. A rare thing in these parts. The paunch, not the limp. Lots of folks hitched when they walked, but few of them had seen enough food over recent years to fill their bellies let alone grow them.

A strange thought occurred to him. Had Mama shacked up with this man? Was Will about to meet a stepfather he'd never known he'd had?

No.

Mama said she'd never marry again.

Still, hard times drove hard choices, and strange times bred strange actions.

Whoever this man was, Will didn't reckon there was any sense in sitting there unarmed while this fella marched closer and closer with his rifle.

Will leaned and pulled the Spencer from its scabbard and laid it across his saddle and turned the mule a little so the muzzle was pointed in the man's general direction.

Forty-five yards away, the man came to a halt. "Just keep on riding, stranger," the man said with no twang to his voice at all. "We ain't got nothing for you here."

"I'm no stranger," Will said, "not to this property. This is my home."

The man blinked at him a couple of times then said, "No, it ain't. It's my home." His voice was pure Yankee through and through, harsh and uptight. "I bought it and hold the deed."

"What are you talking about? My mama and sister live here."

"Would your name be Bentley?"

"That's right. Will Bentley. Now where's my family?"

"I got no idea. No idea at all. They were already gone when I moved in."

"Already gone? Who sold it to you, then?"

"We were riding past, me and my family, and we saw it and went to town and checked, and all I had to do was pay the back taxes, and it was mine, not that that's any business of yours."

Will felt sick. This man had bought the place for back taxes?

Will had heard of things like that happening. Quite a lot, in fact. Especially to families whose members had worn the gray.

Confederate scrip was worthless now, and nobody had any Union money. Folks fell behind on their taxes.

Yankee carpetbaggers were coming down in droves and buying up farms and ranches for pennies on the dollar. All they had to do was pay off delinquent taxes.

But that couldn't have happened here. Will had sent Mama enough money to pay the taxes twenty or thirty times over.

Will eyed the man. "I don't like your attitude, mister."

"Nor I yours. And I don't like you coming onto my property, asking questions."

"I'm not on your property. I'm in the road."

"Good. You keep it that way."

"Or what?"

"Or I'll tell the law, that's what. Sheriff Rickert takes care of folks like you, folks who try to take what's not theirs no more. Escorts them away."

"Rickert? He couldn't escort a fat man to a pie."

"Well, he does. Him and his deputies. And if there's any trouble he can't handle, there are federal troops stationed in town, too."

"I heard about them. Heard they're green as cucumbers."

"That's none of my affair. If you want trouble with the soldiers, you'll have it. But leave me out of it."

Will stared at the man, wanting to push him, wanting the man to give him an excuse to put a bullet in his guts or to get off his mule and go over and beat some manners into him.

It wouldn't take much.

But he had other fish to fry. Namely, finding his mama and rescuing his sister. Besides, he'd heard other stories, stories of Reconstructionists hanging folks who gave Yankees trouble.

Especially ex-Confederates.

So Will just said, "I'll be back, carpetbagger," then turned and rode off with a war drum beating in his chest.

Where was Mama?

If anyone knew, it would be the Dunnes next door. And there wasn't much chance of them losing their farm. They had money, and Mr. Dunne, after arguing against secession, had ridden north and worn the blue.

He'd died halfway through the war, but Will doubted the Reconstructionists would let anyone appropriate the ranch of a Union soldier.

So Will headed down the road, hoping Mrs. Dunne would know where Mama had gotten to. The last Will knew, Mama was still having Bible study with Mrs. Dunne every morning, and Rose was still best friends with the Dunnes' maddening little daughter, Maggie.

A short time later, he rode through the Dunnes' gate and down the long path to their home, cutting through fallow fields with a feeling of dread growing inside him.

Why weren't these fields plowed?

The path upon which he rode had seen very little traffic in recent weeks.

The path passed through a grove of live oaks and out the other side to where the Dunnes' farmhouse stood.

Only there was no farmhouse.

Where it should have been stood only a heap of charred timbers.

It was a punch to the gut. The Dunnes had been nice folks.

Were Mrs. Dunne and her children all right?

Will rode up to the charred remains of the house and dismounted and stared at the devastation.

It was a shame. A darned shame.

The fire had been recent. Weeks ago, not months. Countless hoofprints still marred the scorched earth where raiders had encircled the home.

They'd trampled the vegetable garden. Further from the house, the hog pen stood empty as did the pastures.

Mr. Dunne had always kept a few head of cattle and the nicest horses Will had ever seen. He'd imported them from Kentucky. Prime thoroughbreds with fine lines, far different creatures than the small, tough, cattle horses most East Texans rode.

Gone now. All gone. Everything.

The fields lay fallow. The barn and bunkhouse remained, their whitewash fading and peeling in the bright spring sunlight.

Will dismounted and led the mules over to the water trough. Tired as they were, he just ground hitched them, knowing they would appreciate the water and the shade of the scorched cottonwood.

He stood there for a moment, staring at the place, hoping the Dunnes were okay and wondering how in the world he was going to find Mama, let alone Rose.

Studying the ground, he noticed footprints coming and going over the marks left by the raiders.

He followed these away from the devastation toward the bunkhouse, a glimmer of hope coming to life within him.

Ten feet from the structure, he remembered his manners and called, "Hello, the bunkhouse!"

There was no response. He waited a long time.

A cat wandered out of the barn and flopped down on the gravel to watch him.

Will repeated his call, but still no one answered.

Satisfied that he was alone, he walked forward and opened the door, hoping he might see some sign of whoever had been walking around here lately.

But as soon as he opened the door, he froze in place, his guts turning to ice water.

Two feet away, a double-barreled shotgun was pointed at his face.

CHAPTER 5

The person holding the shotgun was the fiercest-looking, most striking woman he'd ever seen. Framed in locks of thick, deep red hair, her green eyes flashed dangerously, telling him she was ready to pull the trigger and end his life.

And yet he was so mesmerized, so stunned by her beauty, that he felt no fear.

Even her snarl, with its perfect white teeth, was alluring.

Suddenly, that snarl lifted into a smile, and the woman lowered the shotgun. "Will!"

"Yes," he said and stared at her. There was something familiar about her face. Those eyes...

"Why, don't you even remember me, Will? It's me, Maggie."

"Maggie?" he mumbled dumbly. He couldn't help it. How could this lovely woman be Rose's irritating little friend, Maggie Dunne?

Why, when he'd left for the war, Maggie had been a bright-eyed tomboy with a wild streak wider than the Red River, always pestering Will while he was trying to work and getting his sister into a heap of trouble.

"If you don't remember me, Will Bentley," Maggie said—and it was Maggie; he saw that now, saw it in her eyes and the angles of her changed face, saw that she had matured into a woman of unmatched beauty—frowning at him, "I'm going to go ahead and shoot you after all."

"Don't shoot," he said, smiling at her joke. "I remember you, Maggie. It's just you... grew up. I didn't recognize you was all. You look different."

She put her hands on her hips. "You haven't seen me for six years, Will. Did you think I still had pigtails in my hair and frogs in my pockets?"

Then she rushed forward and wrapped her arms around him and kissed his cheek, and he put his arms around her and was surprised to realize he was uncomfortably and involuntarily attracted to this gorgeous young woman who had always before been his little sister's troublesome shadow, a pint-sized pain in the neck with fire in her eyes and laughter in her heart.

Now, however, there was certainly nothing pint-sized or girlish about Maggie. She was all woman. Her firm body filled his embrace, waking something primal in him.

They released each other and stepped apart.

"What happened here?" Will asked. "Where are your folks?"

Maggie bit her lip, and for a second, she no longer looked so grown up. In that instant, she looked more like she had that time, years earlier, when she'd fallen out of the tree and busted her arm.

Rose had fetched Will, and he'd hurried over and picked up the injured girl and carried her back to her house. Maggie had lain in his arms, quivering from the pain and biting her lip, too tough to cry.

"Raiders," she said. "A dozen of them, maybe more. Jafford Teal's gang, riding up out of the thicket. Set fire to the house. They were shooting, too. Killed Mama and Matt and Paul. Burned them up."

"Because of your daddy?"

She nodded. "The war's over, but they're still butchering. What did my mama and brothers ever do to them?"

He laid a hand on her shoulder. "Not a thing, Maggie. Not a thing. Some men are just filled with hate. I'm sorry this happened to you."

"Thank you, Will. I wish you'd been here. You would've driven them off."

Will doubted that. More likely, going up against a group like that, a dozen men bent on destruction, he'd have gotten himself killed, but he didn't bother to say that. If his presence made Maggie feel safer, good.

"They would have killed me, too," she said, "if I hadn't been at your house, tending to your mama and Rose. They were sick as dogs."

"I'm sorry, Maggie. That's just terrible."

He could see the conversation was painful for her, but she smiled anyway. "Your mama took me in then, treated me like family."

"I went next door, looking for Mama, and some man over there says he bought the place."

Maggie nodded. "That would be Mr. Braintree. Carpetbagger. Bought it for the back taxes and kicked us out the very same day."

So it was true, then. The family homestead was gone. His daddy had made it, and Will had kept it going, kept improving on things, until the war came, and he and some other men had gone to Bonham and joined the 5th.

Now the farm was gone. Snatched up by the sort of carpetbagger who would kick out women who had no place to go.

"They've been staying here with me ever since. Then Rose got kidnapped."

"Is she okay?"

"Probably? I don't know, though, honestly. I mean, I couldn't say for sure. I'll let your mama tell it."

"Do you know where Mama is?"

"She's right out back, tending to a second garden we planted back there. Come on. She'll be happy to see you."

CHAPTER 6

They went around the bunkhouse, and there stood his mama, Angela Bentley, five feet, three inches of backbone in blue gingham.

"Mama," he said.

Mama smiled. She was still a good-looking woman despite the hard times and streaks of gray now sparkling in her light brown hair. "Will. I knew you would come back to us. I knew we could count on you."

They embraced. Then Mama stepped back, holding him by the arms, and looked him up and down. "Well, you're ragged and filthy, but you've filled back in since I last saw you. You were thin as a scarecrow when you first came home."

"War'll do that to a man," Will said.

"You need a bath and a change of clothes."

"I have one more set, ma'am, but truth be told, they don't look much better than these. They're cleaner is all."

"Well, if I had the means, I'd make you a new set."

"Thank you, ma'am. You just tell me what you need, and I'll pick it up. I might not have clothes, but I do have some money. What happened?"

Maggie said, "You'd better come on in and sit down, Will." She took him by the arm and led him into the bunkhouse. "We've had a hard time of it."

"Is Rose okay?" he asked.

"We don't know," Mama said, "but I think so."

"Where is she?"

"Isaac Pew took her."

"Isaac Pew?"

Of the many possibilities that occurred to him over the long ride from Colorado, he'd never once considered that his sister might have been kidnapped by a rich old man.

Mama nodded. "He's got your sister locked away and won't let us see her."

"Locked up? Why?"

"He plans to marry her."

"Marry her? Pew? He's an old man."

"He's also a rich man."

"Rose doesn't care about that."

"And Pew doesn't care what Rose thinks. He's made up his mind to marry her. And he's so rich, he can do whatever he wants."

"I don't care how much money Pew has. He can't marry my sister." He pictured old man Pew riding through town in his black carriage, and in the memory, he wasn't alone. "Wait a second. What about Mrs. Pew?"

"That's why he has Rose locked up. He couldn't marry her right away. That would have been polygamy. Mrs. Pew has been

29

on her deathbed."

Will scowled at the notion. What a wicked old man.

"Well, we'd best get Rose before Mrs. Pew passes," Will said.

Mama nodded gravely. "Lord knows, I don't want trouble, but he can't have my baby."

Maggie said, "Things have changed, Will. The law doesn't apply to men like Pew anymore. They do pretty much whatever they want."

Will burned with indignation. "So in this new Texas, a rich man can kidnap a girl and force her to marry him?"

"If he's a skalawag," Maggie said.

"And the girl's brother wore the gray," Mama added. "I'm sorry, Will. I know that's hard to hear, but I want you to know the truth."

Will clenched his fists. "I'm gonna go talk to Sheriff Rickert."

"I've already been. Several times. And Sheriff Rickert has been about as useful as a two-legged mule."

"Well, I'm about to make him useful. And if he doesn't help, I'll go straight to Pew."

CHAPTER 7

Town was mostly shuttered up. A few places had burned. The streets were empty and quiet, except the Red River Saloon, out of which came the somehow sad sound of someone toying tunelessly with the piano. They would play a few notes, fall silent, play a few more from something else, and go silent again.

Will rode on.

He'd left his mules to rest at Maggie's.

She'd been kind enough to lend him Honey, her beautiful buckskin mare, a fine horse that seemed out of place here in post-war Texas. The mare's breeding was apparent in its perfect lines, and that Maggie had trained her well was apparent in the horse's demeanor and every action.

Trailing behind was Winnifred, Rose's mare, because Will was determined to find his sister and take her home.

Will remembered, as a boy, how excited he'd get, coming to

town. It was a rare event. And everything here had always seemed so nice and fancy and full of life.

It had never been much, he now understood, but to a young pig farmer, it had seemed like New Orleans on the Red River.

Here and there, men stood in groups, looking ragged and filthy and sullen like packs of feral dogs.

Will rode on up the street and past the sheriff's office. He didn't feel comfortable leaving the horses unattended, even outside the sheriff's office, not with all these feral-looking men hanging around with their slack jaws and hungry eyes.

Especially because these weren't his horses. He wouldn't risk losing Maggie's beautiful mare. Or Rose's horse. Winnifred was nothing special, as far as horses went, but Rose loved her and had a temper to boot. She'd skin Will alive if he let these men take her horse. After thanking him for saving her, of course.

So he rode Honey down to the livery. He wasn't sure the place would still be in operation, but as he drew close, he saw the corral was chock full of horses.

"Well, look what the cat dragged in," Joe Lennox, the hostler, said when Will came through the door. "Will Bentley."

"Howdy, Mr. Lennox. Good to see you, sir."

"Good to see you, too. Heard a carpetbagger stole your farm."

"Yes, sir. You heard right."

"Bad business that. Happening all over."

Mr. Lennox got up from behind his desk and walked over to the windows and glanced outside and then went to the side door and looked back and forth before adding, "Them Yankees said the war was all about preserving the Union. Hogwash!

They won't be happy till we're all gone, and they got everything."

"You got that right."

Mr. Lennox nodded. "But you gotta watch what you say these days. And personally, I can't complain. You see them horses outside? They're all Yankee horses. Army's got a bunch of soldiers living in the hotel down the street, but they got too many horses for the hotel corral, so they use my place for an overflow."

"They pay you?"

"A little. I make enough to get by. How's your mama faring?"

"She's all right, sir. Thanks for asking. I'll take care of her now."

"That's good, Will. How's your sister?"

"That's why I'm here. Isaac Pew kidnapped her."

Mr. Lennox sat down again with a heavy sigh. "Heard something about that, about him kidnapping some young girl, but I had no idea it was your sister."

"Yeah, it's her. But I'm fixing to get her back."

Mr. Lennox nodded. "You be careful. Pew's got some tough men working for him."

"As soon as I leave here, I'm heading over to the sheriff's office."

Mr. Lennox frowned. "I hope Rickert helps you."

"It's his job."

"Yeah, well, things have changed around here, Will."

"I see that. Whether Rickert helps or not, I'm getting my sister back."

"I wish you luck. I really do. Like I say, Pew's got some tough men on his payroll. Especially that Sheffield. He's a rough character."

"I'll be all right."

Mr. Lennox was silent for a moment. He looked troubled, and Will could tell he had more to say.

Finally, Mr. Lennox said, "Pew's right in with the scalawags. Welcomed the Yankees with open arms. I hope the bluebellies leave you alone."

"I hear most of the Union troops stationing here don't have a lick of experience."

"Seems that way. But they got a detachment of cavalry that rides a circuit across the region, and they're nobody you'd want to mess with. They come through here now and then, and every last one of them looks hard as nails."

"Well, I don't see where rescuing my sister from a kidnapper would be any concern of theirs."

"You wouldn't think so, would you? But be careful. Try not to stir things up."

"Thanks for the warning, Mr. Lennox. I'll try. But Rose is coming home today one way or the other."

He wrapped up with the hostler, who refused payment. "You go talk to Rickert. I wish you luck."

Will thanked him and left the livery and walked down the street to the sheriff's office.

Will pushed through the door and locked eyes with Sheriff Rickert, a gray-haired, tired-looking man who sat there with his boots on his messy desk and his hands folded atop his stomach.

"Will Bentley," Rickert said. "Ain't seen you in some time."

"You know why I'm here."

"Can't help you, Will. If your sister wants to marry Isaac Pew, that's her business, not mine."

"She doesn't want to marry that old coot and you know it."

"I know no such thing. Why just the day before yesterday, I was over to Pew's ranch, and apparently, she's champing at the bit."

"She didn't tell you that."

"No, but Pew did."

"And you believe him?"

Rickert spread his hands. "Pew's a powerful man in these parts. Especially now. His son-in-law is tight with the Yankees. What do you expect me to do?"

"Your job."

Rickert's face reddened at that. He brought his boots off the desk and stood. "I am doing my job."

"Doesn't seem that way to me, Rickert."

Rickert's eyes flared with anger. "You mind your tongue, Will Bentley."

"You start minding this town, I'll mind my tongue. Looks like I gotta take care of this myself."

"Don't you go over there and give Mr. Pew trouble. You hear me, boy? You give him trouble, I'll be forced to haul you in."

Will stared at him in silence.

Sheriff Rickert tried to hold his gaze but looked away after a few seconds.

Will went to the door and twisted the knob.

"Don't do it, Will," Rickert said in a pleading tone. "I don't want to have come after you. You get arrested now, there's no telling what the judge will do to you. They're hanging folks left and right. Especially those who wore the gray."

Will looked back at the so-called sheriff. "I'm in the right here."

"Don't you get it, Will? Right and wrong don't even matter anymore."

"That's where you're wrong, Rickert. Right and wrong always matter. Even if folks want to pretend they don't."

CHAPTER 8

"You come in here, I'll stab you!" Rose shouted, leaning into the desk she'd pushed against the door.

In her free hand, she held the leg of the chair she'd shattered. It wasn't much of a weapon, but its jagged edge would do some damage.

"Please settle down, Miss Bentley," Isaac Pew's voice said. "Everything is already arranged. The preacher is ready for us. Didn't you find your gown satisfactory?"

"I don't find *you* satisfactory," Rose said. "You kidnapped me and held me here against my will. I would never marry you. You're ancient and evil."

"All men are evil," Pew said. "We're born into sin. The preacher can explain that to you after we're married. As to my age, you should be pleased. Think of all you'll inherit in a few years."

"I don't want anything from you but my freedom."

"Enough of your caterwauling, young lady. I won't have any

more of this foolishness. Open that door this instant, or I'm sending Mr. Sheffield in there to get you."

"Anybody comes in here, he's getting stabbed," she promised.

"Very well," Pew said with a sigh. "Mr. Sheffield, if you will, please."

On the other side of the door, Sheffield growled with effort. The door creaked and started moving inward, shoving the desk and Rose slowly, inexorably backward.

When Sheffield's big hand appeared, gripping the door and shoving, Rose released the desk and swung the broken chair leg. Its point plunged into the big hairy hand, which Sheffield whipped out of sight with a yelp of pain.

Then the big man slammed into the door, bellowing with rage, and knocked it wide open, toppling the desk and making Rose scream.

Rose held the makeshift knife in front of her as Sheffield stepped into the room, hand bleeding and eyes blazing.

The white-haired Mr. Pew entered behind him. "That's quite enough of that, my dear. Come now. Put down the weapon, and we'll go outside together."

"Never!" Rose said. "I'd rather die."

"Don't talk that way, treasure," the old man said. "I can't lose two wives in as many days."

"She's not your wife," a deep voice said outside, and as everyone turned, an angel filled the doorway.

At least, he was an angel to Rose.

"Will!" she cried. "You came for me."

"That's right," her brother said. He looked dirty and ragged and tough. He'd filled out over the years. "Let's go home."

"She's not going anywhere," Mr. Pew said. "She's staying here with me forever. We are to be married."

Will glanced at her. "Is that right, Rose? You want to marry this man?"

"No, Will. I do not. I'd sooner die."

"Just what I figured. Come on. Let's go home."

"Mr. Sheffield," Pew said. "Please show this man off the property."

The burly Mr. Sheffield lumbered forward, reaching for Will.

"You lay a hand on me, I'll knock you into the middle of next month," Will said.

Sheffield grabbed Will's wrist.

Will shifted his weight. There was a meaty thud, and Sheffield fell heavily to the floor, out cold.

Only then did Rose realize her brother had struck the man with a short, vicious punch.

"How dare you invade my property and assault my employee?" Pew demanded. "You will pay for this. What's your name?"

"My name is Will Bentley," Will said, stepping forward.

Pew staggered back to the wall and started to reach inside his black suit jacket.

"You pull a weapon on me, you're gonna wish you hadn't," Will said, laying a hand on the butt of the big revolver shoved through his belt.

Pew brought his hand out again. It was empty. He backed up to the far wall and glared at Will, his eyes shining with indignation. "You'll hang for this, Will Bentley."

"Somebody wants to hang me, it'll take some doing," Will said, crossing the room. "Meanwhile, hear this."

His big hand shot out and grabbed Pew by the ear. "You're too old to hit. But I need you to hear what I say. Hear it and remember it."

He twisted Pew's ear, and the vile kidnapper cried out.

"If you ever bother my family again, I will kill you. You understand me, Pew?"

"Yes," Pew cried. "I understand."

"Good," Will said, and released him. He gestured to Rose, who threw down her makeshift weapon and ran to him.

Rose swelled with relief and gratitude. Her brother had come home, praise God, just as she had known he would.

And with Will home, everything would be all right now.

CHAPTER 9

"So much for ending slavery," Will grumbled as they cut through Pew's plantation, heading for town. The fields were full of folks who had recently been emancipated from slavery into sharecropping.

"Well, I sure am thankful that you freed me, Will," Rose side, riding close beside him. "Thanks for saving me. I knew you would."

He nodded. "I'll always do my best to take care of you and Mama. That's what I thought I'd been doing all along. What happened to the money I sent?"

"Gone. All gone."

"What? How?" He understood Confederate scrip had gone worthless overnight, but he'd sent Union money, greenbacks.

"Someone robbed the bank. Then it went belly up. And that was all she wrote."

He burned with anger, thinking of all the work he'd done, all the money he'd sent, to take care of his family.

All gone.

"Who robbed the bank?" he asked.

"Jafford Teal's gang."

"The same ones who killed Maggie's family."

Rose nodded sadly.

Will thought for a second then said, "Mama told me to quit sending money. She made it sound like you had enough."

"Don't blame Mama. That was my idea, telling you that. Folks were having money stolen out of letters."

"How have you been eating?"

"We've been selling Mama's silver."

Will frowned. "That silver is her prized possession. She got it from her mother."

"It's mostly gone now. Every now and then, we take some to town and barter for supplies. That's what Maggie and I were doing when Pew kidnapped me."

Will reached out and rubbed his sister's shoulder. He was proud of her for holding up so well. Proud but not surprised. Rose had always been tough.

"So you know about the farm?" Rose asked.

He nodded. Losing the farm galled him. But there was nothing he could do about it now. "You been staying in the bunkhouse long?"

"A month and a half. Ever since that carpetbagger stole our farm. Before that, Maggie was staying with us."

"It's terrible, what happened to her family. They were good people."

"It was awful. I'm so glad she was with us when it happened, or she would have died, too. But now that you're home, everything will be okay."

He smiled at her but wasn't so sure himself. Yes, he would take care of them. But he couldn't see a way to stay here and make things right. Everything was too broken, and there were too many bad folks running around.

"What would you think about moving someplace?" he asked. "Colorado, maybe."

Rose shrugged. "Sounds good to me. But Mama won't go. Says she can't leave Pa's bones. Or the babies'. Or Texas, either."

"Yeah, I kind of reckoned she'd say something like that."

"Maggie wouldn't want to leave, either. You know her, always the optimist. She thinks things are gonna get better."

"Maybe she's right. But maybe she's not."

They were silent for a while. Coming to Pew's gates, Will looked back to make sure no one was following.

They weren't. Pew had apparently had enough.

For now, anyway.

But a rich man like Pew, he would never let this stand. Pew thought he was entitled to whatever he wanted, Rose included. And he would never forget Will marching in there and taking her from him, not to mention threatening him and twisting his ear.

All while wearing shabby homespun clothes.

That might not seem like an offense to most folks, but the Pews of the world, a man in raggedy, homemade clothes didn't have the right to speak to Pew, let alone twist his ear halfway off.

So there would be trouble.

Oh well. Will was no stranger to trouble, and if someone came for him, whether it was Sheriff Rickert or a posse of hired thugs, he'd be ready for them.

"Speaking of Maggie," Rose said with a sly smile as they turned onto the main road toward town, "hasn't she gotten pretty?"

"She's a good-looking woman. I didn't even recognize her at first. Though in all fairness, she was pointing a shotgun at me."

"What?" Rose laughed.

"I was poking around the place, looking for someone to help me find Mama, and when I opened the bunkhouse door, there stood Maggie, pointing the double-barrel at my face."

Rose threw back her head with laughter.

It made Will feel good to see her enjoying herself. He knew the last few weeks had been an absolute nightmare.

But Rose had adapted quickly.

That was a family trait.

"So are you gonna marry her?" Rose asked, nearly knocking him out of his saddle.

"Marry her?"

"Why not?"

"That's ridiculous."

"Why?"

Will sputtered, having no real answer, then settled lamely on, "I just got home."

"All right. So you just got home. You can marry her in a few days."

He quirked an eyebrow at his grinning sister.

Grinning… but serious.

He could see she meant it.

"Being locked up in Pew's house must've messed up your head, Rose."

"No, it didn't. But it did give me time to think. And since I knew you'd come to save me, I got to thinking that you should marry Maggie."

"She's just a kid," he said.

"If you saw her bathing in the creek, you wouldn't say that," Rose said. "She is all woman now."

Will's face burned at his sister's words.

Rose laughed. "Will Bentley, that's the first time I've ever seen you blush. She's white as milk under those clothes. Whitest skin I've ever seen. Except for a few pale freckles on her—"

"That's enough of that sort of talk," Will said. His voice came out sort of strange and husky.

This made Rose laugh all the harder. When she recovered, she said, "I'm serious, though, Will. You should marry her. You two are perfect for each other."

"I don't even know her."

"Don't know her? Now you're just being difficult. Maggie and I have been best friends our whole lives. You've known her since the day she was born."

"Yeah, well, I don't know her now. All I ever knew was a pain-in-the-neck kid. And she doesn't know me, either. Besides, you're forgetting her end of the deal. A pretty young thing like Maggie wouldn't want to hitch her wagon to somebody like me."

"You're crazy, Will. Maggie loves you. She always has."

"Loved me? She always messed with me while I tried to work."

Rose shook her head. "You don't know the first thing about women, big brother. That's how a young girl shows interest. By teasing."

"You're the crazy one."

"Ask her if you don't believe me."

"I'll do no such thing."

"We'll see. You spend some time around her, you might just come to your senses."

CHAPTER 10

They rode into town, where the feral-looking men seemed to have cleared out. Reaching Pelton's General Store, they hitched their horses and went inside.

"Afternoon, Rose," Mr. Pelton said from behind the counter. The shelves were mostly bare, and there were no other customers in sight, but Will saw that Mr. Pelton had still been keeping everything neat and tidy.

"Good afternoon, Mr. Pelton," Rose said. "You remember my brother?"

Pelton removed his half-moon glasses and smiled. "Well, hello, Will." He came around the corner to shake Will's hand. "I didn't even recognize you at first. Made it through the war in one piece?"

"Yes, sir."

"Well good, good. You back to stay?"

"Not sure."

"Well, I hope you stick around. Times are hard, Will. I don't have to tell you that. You can see it for yourself. But hard times require good men. We got plenty of the other kind around here these days but not enough of the good ones."

Will nodded at that, appreciating the suggestion that he was a good man, but inside, he yearned to leave.

He loved Texas, but things were rough here.

Farther west, in places like Colorado, folks were forging a new land. He longed to join them.

And truth be told, he wanted to do more than build stone walls. Like many men, he had set his desires aside to provide for others, but he still dreamed of exploring the West, staking a claim, and building something on the frontier, something he could pass along to the children he hoped to have one day.

That couldn't happen here, not until Texas rose again.

But further west was a new land of bold possibilities, where men didn't care whether you'd worn the blue or the gray. They cared not for the past but for the future.

That sounded good to Will, about as good as a breath of air might sound to a drowning man.

But for now, he was here, and he had business to take care of, folks to provide for.

He bought some panniers and filled them mostly with food.

Rose was a big help selecting the things they needed. Not just food but also soap and cloth and lamp oil, things they'd been running low on.

"Does Mama have any tea?" he asked.

Rose's eyes swelled at the extravagant notion. "We haven't had tea in years."

So Will added tea to the order and then, on an uncharacteristic whim, got some coffee, too. He loved coffee. And this was real coffee, not chicory, a treat he hadn't allowed himself for a long, long time.

Finally, he added a tin of beeswax and tallow cartridge lube and a wooden box of paper cartridges for the Colt Dragoon he'd taken off the highwayman. He had plenty of ammunition for his other weapons.

Mr. Pelton totaled the bill and announced the sum with an apologetic tone. "That comes to seven dollars and eight cents, I'm afraid. What do you have in trade, Will?"

"Money."

Mr. Pelton's eyes brightened. "Real money? Union money?"

"That work for you?"

"Yes, sir, it sure does," Mr. Pelton said with a smile. "A lot of folks around here don't trust Union money. Using greenbacks feels like fraternizing with the enemy to them, I guess. But I gotta keep food on my own table, and the folks I deal with, they're mostly shipping goods on steamboats loaded up north, and they only want greenbacks, gold, or silver."

"Fair enough," Will said and counted out seven dollars and eight cents. "Thank you, Mr. Pelton."

"Thank you, Will. This is the first actual money I've seen in a spell. If there's anything else I can do for you, anything I can order, let me know."

Will told him he'd let him know, and he and Rose left the store and stepped out into the sunny day, Will feeling good about rescuing her and filling the panniers with food and supplies.

But as they were loading up the goods, the door across the street opened.

Sheriff Rickert stepped outside, leaned back, and stretched

his suspenders, squinting up at the sky, then swept his gaze along the street and saw them.

Sheriff Rickert's eyes went from Will to Rose and back to Will.

The sheriff frowned and shook his head then went back inside.

Rose, who'd already mounted up, hadn't seen the sheriff but noticed her brother's expression. "What is it, Will? What's wrong?"

"Nothing," he said with a smile.

Not yet, anyway, he thought. *Not yet.*

CHAPTER 11

"Do you think Pew will bother us?" Maggie asked that evening, sitting outside the bunkhouse with Will.

Even though it was only dusk, Mama and Rose were already asleep, having finally given in to exhaustion and relief after the happy reunion and the feast the women had prepared.

Despite the simple ingredients, the meal was fantastic. It tasted, Will had concluded after eating so much that his stomach hurt, like home.

"I reckon he'll try," Will said. "Man like Pew, he's used to having his way. We stopped him today."

"You stopped him."

"Well, whatever the case, he'll be angry. He might even feel like he was the victim, not Rose. So yeah, I reckon he'll try something."

Maggie gave a little shudder. Her eyes scanned the surrounding landscape as if searching for attackers in the gathering shadows.

Will realized that this situation was probably dredging up memories and fears for the poor girl, whose family had been burned and shot just a short distance from where they now sat.

"Don't worry," Will said. "Pew will try something, but it won't amount to much. And it won't be tonight."

"Why not?"

"He has no idea where we are. No one does."

"Good. I'll sleep easier knowing that. But someday…"

"Yes, someday, folks will know where we are. But we'll be ready for them."

Maggie smiled. "You don't scare easy, do you?"

"Never saw much sense in it," Will said.

"When Pew does come, what will he do?"

Will spread his hands. "I'm not sure. But he won't come himself. He'll send somebody. My guess is he'll send Sheriff Rickert."

Maggie shook her head. "I used to think highly of Sheriff Rickert, back before the war. Father told us to always ride with the law and not against it."

"That's good advice," Will said, "so long as the law remains the law."

"What do you mean?"

"I mean your daddy was right about sticking to the law. And we are. If Rickert comes out here, defending that old kidnapper, he's not the law, badge or no badge."

"That makes sense. And it makes me feel better." She studied him for a moment. "Did you hate my father?"

"Hate your father?" Will laughed. "No, ma'am. Your daddy was a good man. I thought highly of him."

"But he wore the blue."

"I'm aware of that."

She gave him a playful shove. "You know what I mean."

"Your daddy had his beliefs, and I had mine."

"Father hated slavery."

"I was never a fan myself. Makes no sense, if you think about it, one man owning another."

"I agree, Will. Slavery is an evil institution."

"It is. But Lincoln didn't have to invade the South. Slavery was on its way out. He talks a lot about the Union, but he overstepped his bounds. Diplomacy might've taken longer, but it would've saved an awful lot of lives on both sides."

"Father knew the losses would be terrible. That was another reason he opposed secession. He feared it would tear everything apart."

"It did a pretty good job of it."

"Do you regret wearing the gray?"

Will cocked a brow, looking at her like she was crazy. "Regret wearing the gray? No, ma'am. Not for one second. Not ever."

"I'm sorry, Will. I didn't mean to suggest you should. Not at all. It's just you understood Father's point of view, so—"

"War is a funny thing, Maggie. A funny, terrible thing. Especially this one. Most times, men don't have a choice. They get conscripted and go fight. This war, we had a choice. Your daddy chose the union, I chose home. That doesn't mean I can't understand his perspective or even agree with him on some points. At the end of the day, though, I'm a Texan first and an American second."

"That makes sense," Maggie said. They were quiet for a

moment. Then she asked, "What would have happened if you and Father had met on the field of battle?"

"We would have fought each other," Will said. "Once the sides are drawn up, you're fighting for your life and the lives of your brothers-in-arms. When you're up against an enemy who's trying to wipe you out, you do your best to destroy them. Everything is very simple then, very straightforward. It's survival. But praise God, your daddy and me never found ourselves in that situation."

"I sure am glad. I never could have forgiven you if you'd killed Father. Did you hate it?"

"What, the war?"

"Yes."

Will looked at her. There was something about Maggie that made him want to be straight with her, to tell her everything, but at the same time, he had learned it was utterly futile to discuss war with anyone who hadn't experienced it.

Had he hated the war?

Yes, bitterly.

But that wasn't the whole story.

How could Maggie understand the other side? How could Maggie understand the euphoria of combat, of killing a man who was trying to kill you?

With no experience in such matters, she would interpret such a confession as bloodlust.

And that was not the case. War is a travesty. But it is a complicated travesty. Its nuances are best discussed between veterans… or not at all.

But Will wouldn't lie to her, so he merely said, "I'm glad it's over. I missed home."

She smiled at that. "We missed you, too. I sure am glad you're back, Will."

He smiled back at her, feeling something between them, something warm and exciting, something he had never experienced before. "Thank you for letting my family stay with you."

"They did the same for me after the raiders came."

"Well, now that I'm home, I'll provide for you as if you were my sister."

"That's nice to know." She was quiet for a moment, then smiled slyly. "You don't think of me as a sister, though, do you, Will?"

"No, I don't."

"That's good."

Will felt that thing between them grow stronger. "Why's that?"

"I won't tell you. A girl needs her secrets."

"All right," he chuckled. "You have your secrets."

"For now," she said.

They sat quietly for a time, surrounded by the sounds of the night bugs as darkness fell. With the moon out and distracted as he was by Maggie, Will barely noticed night's arrival.

"So," Maggie said, "is there a Mrs. Bentley?"

"Sure," Will said. "I thought you knew her."

Even in the gloom, Will could see Maggie's face twist with surprise and disappointment. "I do?"

"Sure you know her," he said with a grin. "Mrs. Bentley is Mama's name."

Maggie smirked at him. "Stop teasing. You know what I mean. Are you married?"

"No, ma'am, I am not."

One corner of her pretty mouth lifted slightly. Then she asked, "Engaged?"

"Nope."

"Have a girlfriend waiting on you back in Colorado?"

"Loads of them."

Maggie frowned.

Realizing she had missed his joke, Will said, "I'm just yanking your chain, Maggie. There's nobody back there. Never was."

She cuffed him in the arm. "You quit teasing me, Will Bentley."

"All right. You want the truth of it? I never met any women in Colorado. I was always working. And even if I had time for that sort of thing, I wasn't going to spend money like that. I saved my money in case Mama or Rose needed anything. So no, I never had a woman."

"Good."

"Good?" He grinned at her. "Some friend you are. You want me to live a loveless life?"

"No," she said and turned away from him, facing the darkness. Then she smiled back over one shoulder. "I just don't want you falling for Colorado girls. I'd prefer you look for love closer to home."

Her words and smile were an invitation. He understood that. He just didn't understand exactly what she was inviting him to do or say.

He was drawn to her—powerfully attracted, in fact—and suddenly, he hoped what his sister had said was true, hoped that Maggie, who was no longer a spirited child but a beautiful, intelligent woman, did have feelings for him.

Because he had feelings for her. Powerful feelings.

But what he had told her was true. He had no experience with women. And he hesitated, suddenly knocked off-balance in a way he wouldn't have been by enemies pouring out of the darkness, firing their weapons.

Because combat, he understood. Women, he did not.

Yet.

By hesitating, he let the moment pass. He felt that—and a twang of loss—when Maggie turned back toward him, and asked in different tone, "Does this still feel like home to you?"

"Texas?"

"Texas, here, everything."

"Sitting here, talking to you, listening to the bugs with night coming down, yeah, it feels like home."

She smiled at his words. "It's nice."

"Yes, it is. But things have changed. This isn't the Texas I left behind."

Maggie glanced toward the charred heap that had been her family's home. "No, it's not."

"I do believe Texas will rise again. But I can't see how or when that will happen. The folks with money and power don't want anything to do with the old Texas."

"Will you go back to Colorado, then?"

He shrugged. "I'm a Texan. I plan on living here, having a family here, dying here. But right now, it's hard to make a living here, and the folks in power don't like people like me. If it was up to me, I'd take you all back to Colorado until this blows over."

Maggie brightened. "You'd take me, too?"

"Sure. I said I'd take care of you, didn't I? But it won't happen."

"Why not?"

"You know why not."

"Your mama."

"That's right. Mama won't leave Pa's bones, not unless there's no other choice."

"It's a shame he's buried over there, on that carpetbagger's farm."

"That isn't the carpetbagger's farm. It's mine. He's just holding it for me. I will get it back, you mark my words."

Maggie studied him for a moment. "I believe you, Will. I believe that you will get your old farm back."

"In the meantime, you need someplace better to live than an old bunkhouse."

"We get by."

"I know you do, but you'll have something better. I'll build you something."

"Well, thank you, Will. That's very kind of you."

"Not really," he said, and grinned. "I just don't want to stay cooped up in a bunkhouse with three women."

She laughed prettily. "You know what house I always liked?"

"Which one?"

"The Kitner place."

Will nodded, picturing the property that ran behind his family farm and Maggie's, separated from their land by Curry Creek. He hadn't seen Kitner's spread since before the war but remembered the house well enough. It was small but tidy, nestled at the edge of Kitner's lushly sprawling acreage.

"He's got a nice little place over there," Will said.

"Correction. He did have a nice little place. He abandoned it."

"Why?"

"You remember he used to run cattle?"

"Yeah, other than Mr. Forester, Mr. Kitner had one of the biggest herds around."

"Until the Confederacy confiscated most of his cattle."

Will winced at the thought. Kitner built up a big herd before the war. Just to have it all taken away. And for as many Texans who'd had their cattle confiscated, it seemed like some of that beef would have made it to Will and other sons of Texas during the war. But it hadn't.

"Then Mr. Kitner built up his herd again," Maggie said, "only to have his cattle confiscated by the bluebellies."

"That'd be enough to break a man."

"It was. Mr. Kitner just picked up and left. Said he was through with Texas and through with cattle. Said he was going to head west and try his luck in the mines."

"Hard work."

"No harder than building up two herds and having them stolen out from under you."

"Good point. So who bought the place?"

"Nobody yet, not that I've heard. It's just one more abandoned property as far as I know."

"Well, how come you've been staying here, then? Why didn't you move into the Kitner house?"

"At first, I was over at your place. Then, I don't know… it wouldn't have seemed right."

"Did Kitner say he was coming back?"

She shook her head. "Quite the opposite. Mr. Kitner was

clear on that point. He said he wouldn't come back to Texas for all the money in the world. Said a team of Missouri mules couldn't drag him back."

"So why not sell the property?"

"Who would buy it? Nobody has any money. He probably fell behind on taxes like everybody and just wanted to be shut of the place."

"That's a shame. But I still say you ladies should've moved in. Lot nicer accommodations than your bunkhouse, no offense."

"None taken. Believe me, I'd love to move in there. It's my favorite house I've ever seen. But someone beat us to it."

"Who?"

"I don't know. But I see lights over there sometimes at night, and one evening when I was down at the creek, I looked over and saw a man walking between the house and barn. I have no idea who he was. At that distance, with the sun going down, he was just a shadow."

"When was the last time you saw him?"

Maggie thought for a moment. "I don't know. It's been a while. A week, maybe?"

"Probably just a squatter. Or maybe it wasn't even the same fella you saw those different times. Lot of folks on the move right now. They travel for a while, stop off at a place like that just long enough to make it a pigsty, then hit the trail again."

"Maybe."

"Tell you what," Will said. "If you're interested, we'll take a ride over there tomorrow and have a look."

"I'd like that, Will. I'd like that a lot."

And suddenly, the feeling was upon him again, the sense of

something between them, or the potential for there to be something.

"I'd like it, too, Maggie," he said, and froze there, looking at her, not knowing what else to say or do.

She looked at him. He looked at her. The bugs seemed very loud.

After a few heartbeats, her smile brightened, growing less genuine. "All right, I'd best turn in if we're going to go exploring tomorrow."

"Sounds good. I could use some shuteye, too. I was on the road for a long time."

He started to follow her toward the bunkhouse, but she spun around and put a hand on his chest, stopping him in his tracks.

"Oh no you don't, Will Bentley. Give me a few minutes before you come inside. I have to get out of these clothes and won't have you peeking at me while I'm naked."

Will's face burned like a branding iron. "Oh... I..."

She smiled at him again. "I'm not a little girl anymore."

"I know."

She turned and went to the door with a little sway in her hips, then looked back over her shoulder at him. "Oh really? I'd started to wonder if you'd even noticed."

Then she slipped inside the bunkhouse, leaving him alone in his confusion with that sense of possibilities swirling around him as his inflamed mind imagined what Maggie was doing—and looking like—just beyond that door.

"Pshaw," he said, whacked a palm against his forehead, and strode off through the darkness to get his mind off these things.

A short time later, he reached the bank of Curry Creek and

the end of Maggie's property. On the other side, a hundred yards back from the creek, was the dark shape of the Kitner place.

But it wasn't completely dark, Will realized, seeing the faint shimmer of light from within the house. Someone in there had a coal oil lamp turned low.

Who are you? Will wondered, and at that instant, as if the man inside had heard Will's thoughts, the light went out.

He had half a mind to sneak over and take a look.

But no. That would be a good way to get shot, and he did not want to get shot again.

He'd wait until morning then mosey over and introduce himself. Which still might be dangerous. There were a lot of folks moving through the country these days. Desperados, some of them. Thieves, murderers, rapists.

He should insist that Maggie stay behind.

But even as the thought occurred to him, he couldn't help grinning. Because he sensed that Maggie still had just enough of that wild, exasperating child left in her to refuse any such suggestion.

They would go together then.

The notion did not bother him.

CHAPTER 12

Sullivan "Sully" Weatherspoon turned from his beautiful black stallion and regarded the slovenly hostler with contempt. "My stallion will have an apple, Lennox, and be sure to quarter it before you feed it to him. That horse is worth more than you'll make in your lifetime."

"Yes, sir," the hostler said.

"And do keep an eye, Lennox. If you allow anyone to steal my stallion, I'll have your hide off and nailed to the wall by sunset."

"Yes, sir, Mr. Weatherspoon, sir," Lennox said with an irritating sigh. A year ago, the hostler had been thoroughly timid. But ever since he'd landed the contract to care for those Union soldiers, he'd lost most of his fear. Sadly, regular food and security brought out the insolence native to all underlings.

Maybe Sully would have to get Roy Gibbs to pay Lennox a visit, remind him of the natural order around here.

Of course, then the hostler might go crying to Captain Culp, and that Sully could not afford. Not now, not after the stunt his cousin just pulled.

Carter Weatherspoon, eighteen years old, had always admired Sully, almost worshipped him. To Carter, Sully could do no wrong, and ever since they were kids, Carter hung around, trying to act like Sully.

It was tiresome, sometimes, having someone follow you around and treat you like a hero, but Sully supposed it was natural enough.

After all, other than his own father, Sully was the most respected man in these parts, especially now that the war had removed so many of the low-born pretenders.

And there had been a certain satisfaction in watching young Carter Weatherspoon swagger among children his own age. Part of that was breeding, of course—and Sully believed in breeding—but mostly, it came down to Carter learning leadership from Sully.

Of course, none of that mattered now, not after the unbelievably foolish thing Carter had done coming out of the saloon the night before.

Drunk as he was, Carter had walked straight into a Union soldier and almost knocked him over.

Which would have been bad enough. But then Carter started insisting the soldier apologize.

The soldier stood his ground, also demanding an apology. Carter was the one, after all, who'd come out of the saloon and slammed into the passing soldier.

Besides, the soldier had another bluebelly with him. And this was their town now.

Voices were raised. Carter, emboldened by whiskey and the presence of his admiring friends, shoved the man.

The soldier cursed and swung a haymaker.

Carter ducked the blow and counterpunched, knocking the man out cold.

This was a colossal blunder on Carter's part, of course. Texans were getting hung for similar altercations. But what happened next made things infinitely worse.

The other soldier went for his pistol, demanding that Carter put his hands up.

Instead of complying, Carter went for his pistol, too.

Both men fired.

According to eyewitnesses, the soldier grazed Carter's arm.

Carter's round punched through the soldier's leg, breaking it, and dropped the man to the ground, where he nearly bled to death before someone applied the tourniquet that saved his life.

Carter fled and hadn't been seen since.

The whole thing was a mess.

Sully's father had been livid, spelling out the various ways that his nephew's actions could destroy the family name and fortune.

So he'd sent Sully to town with a thick envelope of money to smooth things over with the new post commander, Captain Alexander Culp.

Sully headed toward the sheriff's office to see if Rickert had any news. Probably not. The man was utterly useless. But still, Sully wanted to check before talking to Captain Culp.

Sully walked down the street past the saloon, avoiding the bloodstained boards out front, and carried on toward Ricker's office. He came to the mercantile and was just getting ready to cross the street when he spied the detestable Mr. Isaac Pew standing in front of the sheriff's office.

He'd heard strange rumors about Pew lately, something about him kidnapping a girl then letting her get away from him. Now the old man was pacing back and forth in front of the sheriff's office, muttering angrily to himself.

Sully looked away and walked briskly on by, deciding he'd just come back to the sheriff's office later and avoid having to talk to the weird old man.

After passing two blocks of boarded-up and burned-out buildings, he came to the only other shop open on this side of town, Gleason's Café.

The place was empty as usual. Sully took a seat near the window, patted the envelope of money in his pocket, and stared out the window at the street.

"Mr. Weatherspoon," said the proprietor, a homely young woman whose name Sully could never remember. "I'm so glad you're here."

"Six eggs," he said. "You know how I like them. Two slices of toast, buttered, and bacon burnt to a crisp. And coffee."

"Sir," the woman said and looked around, as if wanting to make sure they were alone. "I have something important to tell you."

"Did you get my order?" Sully demanded with irritation.

"I did, sir, but there's something I think you might want to know."

Sully blinked at her. "What in the world could you possibly know that would be of interest to me?"

"Your cousin, sir," the woman said with a smile. "It's about your cousin."

Sully sat up straight. "Do you know where he is?"

She nodded, her smile faltering a little. "He's hurt, sir. He's been asking for you. He needs you. You're the only one who can help him now."

"Where is he?"

The maddening smile returned. "Well, last night, I was just getting ready for bed when I heard a tapping at my window."

Sully grabbed her arm and squeezed. "Where's Carter?"

"Ouch, you're hurting me, sir."

"Tell me where he is."

"He's in the root cellar, sir, wanting to see you."

"Take me there."

She led him into the back of the restaurant, where she pushed aside a stack of potato crates and revealed a door in the floor.

Sully's cousin lay in the shallow space, nearly filling it, and blinked pitifully up at him, squinting in the light. All the swagger had gone out of Carter. Now he was filthy and frightened, one sleeve dark with blood. The reports of his having been "grazed" had clearly underestimated the damage he'd taken. Carter's other hand gripped the revolver he'd used to cause so much trouble.

Seeing Sully, Carter gave a whimper and holstered his weapon. "Sully, you came. I knew you'd come."

"Yes, I'm here. You're okay now."

"I knew I could count on you, Sully. We might be cousins, but I've always thought of you as a big brother. I knew that—"

"Enough talk," Sully said, his mind racing. "You just take it easy, Carter. I'll be back soon."

Carter's eyes swelled with panic, and he started to come out of the hole. "Wait, Sully. Don't leave me."

"Hush now," Sully said. "What if somebody comes in off the street and hears you?"

Carter shot out a hand and latched onto Sully's boot. "Don't leave me, Sully. Get me out of here."

"I'll get you out of here. I promise you that. But first, I must fetch the doctor. You're wounded."

"I can ride."

Sully shook his head. "How long have you been lying in that filthy cellar?"

"All night. I couldn't make it to my horse, and there were soldiers everywhere, and then I saw Alma's light on, and came here."

Alma, Sully thought. *That's her name.* "Well, I'm glad you did and glad Alma was kind enough to take you in."

"I'll always help a Weatherspoon, sir," Alma said. "Besides, I hate them bluebellies. My pa and all three of my brothers got kilt in the war."

"Pity," Sully said flatly. "Now, Carter, you do as I say and just keep hiding where you are. I need to fetch the doctor. He can clean the wound and give you some medicine to make sure you don't get an infection. Once we hightail it out of here, there's no telling when we'll be able to stop running again."

"You mean," Carter said, a huge smile spreading across his dirty face, "you're coming with me?"

Sully smiled back at him. "Of course. Like you said, we're more like brothers than cousins. And brothers stick together through thick and thin, right?"

"You have no idea how happy it makes me to hear you say that... brother."

"You lay still. I'm going to fetch the doctor. Alma, you stay with him. Close the door and cover it with those crates again. I'll be back shortly."

As Sully strode up the street, everything in him tightened with purpose. Now was the time, he thought, that his every move, his every word, mattered. Only by performing perfectly could he save the day.

And that was the difference between him and other men. When the pressure was on, when stakes were high, he never lost his head, never weakened, never failed.

"Mr. Weatherspoon," Isaac Pew said, blocking his path.

The interruption aggravated Sully. He couldn't afford it. But at the same time, Pew was wealthy enough that Sully couldn't just ignore him, either.

"Good morning, Mr. Pew. My condolences on the passing of your wife. She was a good—"

"Yes, yes," Pew said impatiently, brushing the air with one gloved hand. "Where is the sheriff?"

"I don't know, sir."

"Well, I'll tell you where he *should* be. He should be here. This is his office, isn't it? And it's past nine. He should be here, in his office, doing his job."

"Yes, sir," Sully said, and he had the sudden urge to shove the crazy old man aside, to shove him to the ground, in fact, and stomp him a few times for good measure.

But that would not do, of course. Pew held enormous wealth, and besides, in this new Texas, one must be careful. Very careful.

So it was with an apologetic tone that Sully said, "I don't mean to rush by you, sir, but I'm on urgent business."

"As am I," Pew declared, his eyes wild with impatience and madness. "I need to see Sheriff Rickert. If he isn't here in ten minutes, I'll have his badge. You just see if I don't!"

"Yes, sir," Sully said pleasantly. "Good luck, sir."

And he was just walking around Pew when the old man said something that stopped Sully in his tracks.

"I'll see that Will Bentley hang! You just see if I don't!"

Sully's muscles went rigid. Instantly, fury burned bright within him. "Did you say… Will Bentley?"

"That's right. Do you know him?"

Did Sully know him? Oh yes, he knew him. And if there was one man in the world he longed to destroy, it was Will Bentley, the man who had humiliated him and then, later, in a place far from home, witnessed Sully's secret shame, the secret shame that could destroy everything Sully had worked so hard to achieve.

But crafty as he was, Sully had already recovered to a degree, enough to hide his true emotions and face Pew with his mask of good-natured innocence still intact. "I've heard the name."

"He's a savage! He trespassed on my estate, battered my employee, and assaulted me… in my own home. He'll hang. You just wait and see if he doesn't!"

"Well, I'll keep an eye out for him, sir. Now, if you'll excuse me."

Pew launched into another tirade, but Sully turned his back and strode off.

Will Bentley had returned. This was a complication Sully

hadn't seen coming, a complication that put him at risk but also presented interesting opportunities... the chance to have his revenge and finally put to rest any fears of that other, unfortunate matter ever coming to light and ruining his name.

Again, he would have to take his time, plan carefully, and act decisively... just as he must act decisively to save this day.

Walking straight past the doctor's office, he patted the breast pocket where he felt a comforting lump: the money his father had given him to bribe the new Union officer, Captain Culp.

Reaching the hotel, Sully was stopped by a pair of rifle-toting negros in Union blue.

Most of the occupational forces were black men. Every Texan knew this was a taunt to former slave owners, salt in a still gaping wound.

But Sully smiled genuinely, thinking how angry the men now demanding to know his business would be if they knew all the things he had done to his slaves, the things he was still doing to the so-called servants still living on his plantation.

"Good morning, gentlemen," he said. "Is the captain available?"

After answering some questions and surrendering his weapons, Sully was led inside, where he waited for a short time before being escorted into the office of the new post commander, Captain Alexander Culp, a cadaverous man with a hard face and suspicious eyes.

"What is it?" Captain Culp demanded.

Sully introduced himself.

Culp was not impressed. "Why are you here?"

"I have something of value to you," Sully said, and thought of the many drinks and women he might buy with the money hidden inside his clothing.

"Something of value, eh?" Captain Culp said. "Let me be straightforward with you, Mr. Weatherspoon. I know your name. I knew it before I assumed this post. And if you think you can bribe me…"

"Bribe you?" Sully said, feigning shock.

Which, truth be told, wasn't difficult.

Because Sully was surprised. How did the captain know his name? What would this mean over the coming months? And most concerning of all, was Captain Culp bluffing, hoping for bigger paydays than his predecessor, or was he actually that rarest and most detestable of things: an honest man?

The notion confounded and alarmed Sully, but he shoved it aside for later consideration. Because regardless of the captain's true nature, his words had played perfectly into Sully's plan.

And now, it was time to save the day.

"Captain, you have figured me all wrong. I am not here to bribe you."

Culp looked dubious. "Nothing you can say will save your cousin, Mr. Weatherspoon. And yes, I am aware that Carter Weatherspoon is your cousin. We will bring him to justice, and he will pay for his crime. Under my watch, Mr. Weatherspoon, no one is above the law."

Sully didn't like the sound of that. But he smiled nonetheless. "I'm happy to hear that, sir, because I am here to help you. Carter Weatherspoon is gravely wounded and hiding in the back of Gleason's Café. The owner, a woman named Alma, hid him in the root cellar beneath a stack of crates."

The captain's suspicious eyes narrowed further. "You're turning in your own kin?"

"Yes, sir," Sully said with what he intended to be an ingratiating smile. "I stand with you, Captain Culp. I stand with law and order... always. And please tell your men to be cautious. Carter has a revolver and might try to shoot his way out of there. He's desperate and delusional."

CHAPTER 13

☙

"You two sure you don't want to join us?" Will asked.

"No thanks," Rose said. She was slumped at the table, nursing a cup of coffee. "Guess the whole thing is finally catching up to me. I feel like going back to bed."

"And I'll stay here with her," Mama said with a smile. Was that an amused glimmer in Mama's eyes? "You two have fun."

"Thanks, Mrs. Bentley," Maggie said.

"How many times have I told you, child? Call me Mama."

"Yes, Mama," Maggie said.

Will studied his mother's face for a second. Yes, there was no doubt about it. She was having fun. Sly fun. Something about Will and Maggie.

What did Mama suspect? What did Mama know?

"Ready, Mr. Bentley?" Maggie said cheerily.

"Almost. You have any weapons?"

"I do not," Maggie said. "Our guns burned in the fire."

"We still have the shotgun you gave us before heading to Colorado," Mama said. "She can borrow that."

"Thank you, Mama," Maggie said and retrieved the shotgun from where it leaned beside Mama's bunk.

Will was pleased to see Maggie break open the double-barreled coach gun and check the loads.

Out of habit, he checked his own arsenal: the .44 caliber 1860 Colt Army Model revolver; the Dragoon of the same caliber, which he'd taken off the highwayman; his fourteen-inch Confederate Bowie knife; his seven-shot .56-.56 Spencer rifle; and the thirteen-cylinder Blakeslee box, which weighed nine pounds and held ninety-one rounds of ammunition that he could load with lightning speed.

"Loaded for bear, aren't you, son?" Mama asked. "You expecting trouble over there?"

"No, ma'am," Will said. "Not really. But I did see a light over there last night, so there's no telling. Better safe than sorry. Speaking of which, here." He handed Mama the Dragoon. "No sense you being unarmed while we're away."

"I wish I'd had the shotgun the day Pew kidnapped me," Rose said. "Would've gotten home a lot sooner."

"Home or hung," Mama said. "It's best to leave men like Pew alone these days. Same goes for folks like the Weatherspoons. You hear me, Will?"

"Yes, ma'am, I do. Don't worry. I have no plans of starting trouble with anybody, not even snakes like Sully Weatherspoon."

"Good. Because that is trouble we do not need."

"Go ahead and ride Winnie," Rose said. "No self-respecting cavalryman should be seen riding a mule."

"Normally, I'd defend my mules from a comment like that, dear sister, but seeing as how they're worn to a nub, I'll take you up on your offer and give them a break. We might end up riding around the property some, so don't worry if we're gone for a while."

"Oh, you two young folks take your time," Mama said, and there was that amused look again.

This time, Rose giggled, and Maggie blushed bright red.

"Am I missing something here?" Will said.

"I hope not," Rose said. "I really hope you don't miss anything," and this time, it was Mama's turn to laugh.

Maggie blushed all the brighter.

"Come on, Maggie," Will said. "These two have a case of the giggles. Let's get out of here."

They went outside and mounted up and rode across the property.

Maggie rode well. She always had. She didn't just ride well. She was a great trainer, too. Even as a child, she had all her father's horses doing tricks. At ten, she could make them bow, kiss, jump, or rear up on her call.

The Dunnes were horse people, and Maggie had been riding since shortly after she could walk. When she was little, she'd driven her family crazy by racing and jumping and acting thoroughly unladylike, but now she rode with poise, her long, red hair fluttering like bright flames behind her.

For a second, Will could only stare, drinking in her beauty, studying every line of her perfect face, admiring her Roman nose, emerald eyes, and full lips.

"It's impolite to stare, Mr. Bentley," Maggie said, turning toward him.

Will's face went hot with embarrassment.

Maggie laughed. "It's okay, Will. I don't mind you staring at me. I hope you like what you see."

He grinned, knocked off-balance by her forward comment. It seemed that behind the beautiful features into which Maggie had matured, a good deal of the mischievous child he'd known still lurked.

"Come on," she said, "I'll race you to the creek!"

And without waiting for his reply, she spurred Honey, and the magnificent buckskin galloped off, pitching divots of soft earth into the air.

Will raced after her, but Winnie was no match for Honey, and Maggie beat him by several lengths and leapt the creek in a single bound.

She wheeled around and waited for him, laughing and bright-eyed, her face full of color and excitement.

Drawing rein, Will stared again, taking in her happy face, figuring this was a moment worth remembering, a time he would never forget, no matter how long he lived.

Then, as if sensing Will's thoughts and wanting to stamp this moment onto his memory, Maggie said, "Kick the sky, Honey."

Instantly, the beautiful mare reared up, kicking with her front hooves.

"You always were good at training horses," Will remarked.

Maggie smiled. "I enjoy working with horses. I trained all of Father's horses, especially Bastion, his prize stallion. No matter what I said, Bastion obeyed. It used to drive Father crazy. He would be riding, and I'd call Bastion, and the stallion would come running to me and do whatever I told him to do, not matter how much Father hollered."

She shook her head, laughing. "I guess I really was a little mischievous as a girl."

"A little?" Will said.

"Like this one time—it happened right here, come to think of it—I called Bastion over, and Father told me to stop, and as a joke, impulsively, I told Bastion to kick the sky, and he reared up, and Father wasn't ready and fell into the creek. I got in big trouble that time."

They had a good laugh over that.

But behind this beautiful woman stood the Kitner house, and after crossing the creek, Will swept the property with sharp eyes accustomed to hunting for danger.

The change in him frightened Maggie. "What is it, Will? What do you see?"

"Nothing," Will said, "but we'd best be careful from here on out. No telling who's been shacking up here."

As he started forward, Maggie brought Honey close to Winnie, so close that Maggie's leg brushed against Will's.

If there was trouble, they would be safer spread apart, but Will didn't point this out. He liked the feel of her leg against his.

Some risks are worth taking.

Will went slowly, studying everything, including the ground before them.

"Hello, the house!" he called, reining in fifty feet from the structure.

There was no response.

A breeze passed, stirring the tall weeds surrounding the home.

He repeated his call. Waited.

Still nothing.

"Nobody's there, I guess?" Maggie said.

"Maybe. Or maybe they're hiding in there. And maybe they've got their crosshairs on us."

Maggie rode close, her thigh pressing firmly into his.

When they reached the dirt lane that led to the house, Will stopped and studied its surface. It was what he would have expected from a path leading to an abandoned property, all hardpacked earth and weeds growing up.

Which was strange, given that someone had been inside just the night before.

He scanned the grass to either side of the path but saw no signs of horses having passed.

Perhaps the squatter had no horse. Perhaps he had walked here from wherever he had last taken up residence.

Or *they*, Will reminded himself. There could be a whole slew of folks staying here.

"Hello, the house!" he called again.

Silence.

He moved in a slow circle around the home, calling out from time to time and getting no response.

When he reached the back of the place, he finally saw tracks where someone had been walking back and forth between the house and barn.

"Hello, the barn!" Will called and, getting no response, approached with caution that turned out to be unnecessary.

The barn was empty.

But there were fresh horse droppings in one stall, and it only took a minute to read the signs from there.

"Whoever he is," Will said, "he's been avoiding the main road. See? He's been cutting across the back lot, avoiding folks."

Maggie nodded, looking unsettled. "Do you think he's an outlaw?"

"Could be. But might not be, too. Lots of folks on the move these days, and I reckon most are in no hurry to be seen. One way or the other, I'm not worried about it."

Maggie smiled. "Neither am I, then. When I'm with you, I feel safe."

"Good. But you keep that shotgun handy just in case."

They dismounted and ground hitched the horses and knocked on the door and went inside.

Whoever had been staying here had taken good care of the place. He had left no personal items but had made his mark by sweeping the floors and setting wood in the fireplace.

Maggie noticed, too. "Well, whoever's been staying here isn't a slob, anyway."

Will nodded. "I stopped by a few abandoned places on my way home, and they were all torn up. Mud tracked all over, rotting food on the tables, trash on the floor. Most times, folks had busted up the furniture to burn instead of bringing in proper firewood."

"Well, our visitor seems to be a well-mannered guest," Maggie said.

"He does indeed," Will agreed, but inwardly, he knew that meant nothing. Some of the deadliest men he'd ever known were fastidiously, even compulsively clean, and most good soldiers understood the value of keeping their gear and base in good order.

"I sure would love a house like this," Maggie said, drifting from room to room, having finally relaxed enough to do what she'd set out to do. "Come on, Will, let's explore the upstairs."

"All right. But I hope our guest doesn't come back while we're up there. Think of the scandal."

She paused at the entrance of the stairs. "You're going to mind your manners aren't you, Mr. Bentley?"

"Of course, Miss Dunne."

"Then let there be a scandal," she laughed and disappeared through the door. "It'll make us the most interesting figures in the county."

Will shook his head. She was something. Really something. Then he followed her upstairs and, as promised, behaved himself while they went from room to room.

It didn't take long. There were only three rooms, two small and one large. All three remained furnished.

The visitor had been staying in the big bed in the main room.

Not that he'd messed things up. Quite the opposite.

The big bed was neatly made and clean. The beds in the other two rooms were blanketed in dust.

"I can't believe how much Mr. Kitner left behind," Maggie said, when they went back downstairs.

"Guess he really meant it about being finished with Texas," Will said.

"Part of me agrees with him," Maggie said. "Part of me wants to ride off and never come back. But part of me knows this is where I belong. That part wants to stay and ride this out, make it work."

"I feel the same way," Will said. "There's a heap of trouble here. But it's home, trouble or not. And let's face it, when have Texans known anything but trouble?"

They studied the outside of the house and took their time looking over the barn and other outbuildings. There was a well between the house and barn.

"I love this place," Maggie said.

"It's nice."

"Really nice. Want to ride around the property?"

"If we're gone too long, Mama and Rose might think we're up to something."

"Let them," Maggie said, climbing onto Honey. "Rose will be delighted. I suspect Mama will be, too."

And then, without waiting for his reply, she rode off across the open field.

CHAPTER 14

They spent the morning riding around the Kitner place. It was a nice-sized spread, over a thousand acres, anyway, and maybe even two full sections, Will reckoned.

Whatever the exact dimensions, the land was beautiful with plenty of water and grass and some timber and a small quarry out of which Kitner had only just begun to pull stone.

The quarry was one more sign of how ambitious Kitner had been. He had fenced much of the property, too, and built sturdy corrals close to the house and barn.

For as beautiful as the property was, however, it paled beside Maggie's loveliness.

She mesmerized Will. She truly did.

It wasn't just her pretty face, flowing red hair, and well-formed figure that made her so attractive. It was her voice, too, the sound of it and the things she said and the way her face lit up when she laughed, which she did often.

He also appreciated her physical grace, which became

clearer and clearer as they rode side by side. Whether they raced across open ground, leapt over obstacles, or wove slowly through groves of oak and cottonwood, she rode as well as he if not better. Which was saying something, since he was a veteran cavalryman, and one who'd rarely met his match on horseback. But Maggie rode like a centaur, and it pleased him immensely.

When the sun had passed its apex and started toward the West, they finally headed for home. Reaching the creek, Maggie paused and looked back toward the lonely white house and acres of gorgeous pastureland.

"Well, I've made up my mind," she joked. "It suits my needs. You may buy me this ranch."

"All right," he said, and they crossed the creek and were on her property again.

"Thanks for bringing me along, Will," she said, brushing her thigh against his again. "I had a nice time."

"So did I."

They returned to the bunkhouse and chatted easily as they took care of the horses. Maggie did most of the talking, reminiscing about the past and giving him a hard time for being so stern and serious when she was little.

"You were no fun," she complained.

"And you were a pain in the neck."

"Do you still feel that way?"

He grinned at her. "That has yet to be determined. You still seem a bit mischievous."

"You have no idea, Mr. Bentley." Maggie stuck her tongue out at him then ran, laughing, from the stable.

Will chuckled and walked after her. He was just in time to see her disappear into the bunkhouse.

He paused for a moment, thinking about Maggie. She sure was something.

Was it possible that Rose had spoken the truth? Was it possible that Maggie had feelings for him?

Unbelievably enough, it seemed that way. All morning and the night before, she had been friendly... and more than friendly. She seemed excited to spend time with him. She laughed easily and talked freely and seemed to like being close to him.

He remembered the feel of her thigh against his and how excited he'd been to find himself in the bedroom with her, standing inches apart and surveying the big room and its neatly made bed.

Throughout all the time they'd spent together, he'd felt that thing between them, drawing them closer, forming something... and the more he felt it, the more he wanted to feel it.

Looking around at the bunkhouse and burnt home beyond, he wished he'd come home sooner. He hated that his family and Maggie had been living this way.

Oh well. There was no way to change that now. But he wouldn't let them live this way much longer.

Going inside, he told them he was going to go to town to pick up a few things. "Anybody need anything?"

The women looked at each other.

"Don't be shy," Will said. "We have money. Make out a list, and I'll get everything I can. Mama, if you don't mind, I'll borrow your mules and wagon. I want to stop at the hardware store, too, for lumber and other things."

"May I come with you?" Maggie blurted. "I haven't been to town since... well, you know."

She glanced at Rose, who said, "Yeah, I know, and you two have fun, but I won't be joining you. I'm in no hurry to head back there."

"I'll stay with Rose," Mama said, that amused look coming onto her face again.

"Do you mind, Will?" Maggie asked.

"No, you can ride shotgun."

"The bandits won't stand a chance," Maggie laughed.

"You two had better eat first."

Will started to say he wasn't hungry, but the women fussed until he finally gave in and sat down and ate a plate of food.

Then they were finally on their way.

As before, it was a joy to spend time with Maggie. She rode close beside him on the wagon seat, her body touching his, and talked pretty much nonstop all the way to town.

In town, there were a lot of people on the streets, and Will tensed as he passed half a dozen bluebellies on horseback.

"Are you okay?" Maggie asked, laying a hand on his thigh.

"Yeah, I'm all right."

"Does it bother you, seeing Union soldiers?"

"I'm all right."

"I know you're all right, Will, but I can also tell you're tense. It must be strange, after four years of fighting Union troops, to see them here."

"I hate it," Will said, honestly. "I hate seeing them here in my hometown."

"I don't like it myself, even though my own father wore the blue. They don't belong here."

"No, they don't," Will said. He realized, despite the mild weather, he had broken out into a sweat.

It wasn't fear. Far from it. Those men were raw recruits who barely knew a butt from a muzzle let alone how to fight from horseback.

Besides, Will had rejected his fear as a nine-year-old boy, rejected it wholesale as part of the vow he'd made to his dying father. If he was to be the man of the house, he couldn't afford to be frightened like a little kid.

Only later, when he went off to war and saw soldiers unmanned by fear, did he realize how rare that was.

So no, he did not fear these bluebellies. His body had broken out in a sweat because seeing them triggered his fighting instincts. After four years of doing his best to put bullets through the buttons of those blue uniforms, he felt tense and edgy and ready for a fight.

"Aren't you going to stop at the mercantile?" Maggie asked when he rode past. "Later," he said, enjoying her confusion, which helped put the bluebellies out of mind.

"Oh, you're starting at the hardware store," she guessed.

"Nope. Something else."

"What?"

"You'll just have to wait and see. A man's got to have his secrets."

Maggie laughed and bumped into him.

A short while later, she said, "I wonder why there are so many people out."

Will stopped and helped Maggie down and secured the horses and wagon and asked a passing man, "What's with all the people? Something going on?"

"You missed it," the man said. "Last night, a fella named

Weatherspoon got in a fight with a bluebelly then shot another one. They just apprehended him over at the café."

Will grinned. "Weatherspoon? Sully Weatherspoon?"

"No, sir. A cousin of his, I think. Carter's the name."

"Oh well," Will said. "Better luck next time."

The man looked at him strangely and moved on.

Will led Maggie in the other direction.

"Too bad it wasn't Sully," Maggie said. "He gave me an awful time back before the fire."

Something rose in Will then, a savage darkness, fierce and possessive. "What do you mean, he gave you a hard time?"

"Oh, he got it in his head that he was going to court me. I wasn't interested. He didn't like that."

"He didn't try to force anything, did he?"

"Not exactly. I mean, he just wouldn't give up, no matter how clear I made it. He would tell me that I was going to marry him, I just didn't know it yet, that sort of thing. He even started coming to the farm. That was the final straw. My brothers stepped out with their guns, and I told Sully exactly what I thought of him."

Maggie laughed, but he could tell the memory troubled her.

"I wasn't very nice," she confessed. "It really bothered him. You should have seen his face. He looked like he wanted to kill me."

"He's mean by nature and used to having his way," Will said. "Was that it, then? Did he leave you alone?"

She nodded. "Yes, that was the last I heard of him." She smiled sadly. "Of course, Teal's raiders burned us out a couple of weeks later. Maybe Sully thought I died. Maybe that's why he's left me alone. I haven't seen him since."

"You don't have to worry about Sully Weatherspoon, not with me home," Will said and stopped in front of the county office.

"What are we doing here?"

"You'll see," Will said, opening the door for her.

Inside, they were greeted by Jasper Blevins, the county clerk. "Well, hello, Will. I ain't seen you in a coon's age. And would that be Miss Dunne?"

"It would," Will said, shaking the man's hand. "Mr. Blevins, meet Maggie Dunne. Maggie, Mr. Blevins."

Mr. Blevins smiled. "I haven't seen you for years, not since well before the war, when you were just a little girl, but I'd recognize that hair of yours anywhere. If I recall correctly, the last time I saw you, you were in trouble for crawling halfway into the pickle jar over at the general store."

Maggie burst out in laughter. "Oh yes! I remember that. But I didn't just crawl halfway in. I fell in! Then we came in here because Father had to pay the taxes, and he made me stand close to the door because I smelled like pickles."

Mr. Blevins slapped the counter, laughing hard. "That's it. That's exactly what happened. Well, I'm glad to see you again, Miss Dunne, and I was sorry to hear about your family."

"Thank you, Mr. Blevins," Maggie said. "I miss them."

"I'll bet you do, young lady. Horrible thing. I hope someone shoots that Teal soon. He claims to still be fighting the war. He's not fighting the war, unless he's waging it against Texans. He's a murdering thief, that's what he is. I hope somebody shoots him dead."

"So do I, Mr. Blevins," Maggie said.

"But here I go, spoiling things. You folks came in here with smiles on your faces. Let's just forget Teal and all the rest of it. Now, what can I do for y'all?"

"We're back for the same reason that Maggie was here last time. What are the back taxes on her property?"

"Just a moment, and I'll look that up for you, Will. Gosh, it's good to see you again. You've grown. Filled in with muscle." Blevins turned his spectacles toward Maggie. "Have you ever seen such muscles on a man?"

"Nope," Maggie said with a grin. "Never. Will's muscled up like a fine stallion."

Embarrassed, Will said, "Let's see about those back taxes."

While Mr. Blevins fetched his book, Maggie said, "It's fun to watch you squirm."

"You liked that, huh? Better watch out or I'll dunk you in Pelton's pickle barrel."

She laughed and bumped her hip into his. "What are we doing here? Even if the back taxes are ten cents, I can't pay them."

"Hush," Will said, "or it's the pickle barrel for you."

Laughing, she bumped her hip into his again. "You wouldn't dare, Will Bentley."

"Don't tempt me," he said, and then Blevins came back with his book.

"Well, the taxes haven't been paid for a few years. Of course, the county absolved taxpayers of all liability for two years running, so the total back taxes owed are sixteen dollars and fourteen cents."

Will took out his wallet and retrieved a stack of greenbacks.

Mr. Blevins smiled, and his eyes swelled behind his spectacles. "You have money."

"That is correct."

"Excellent," Mr. Blevins said. "And you wish to pay the taxes in full?"

"Yes, sir," Will said.

"That's wonderful, Will. Give me a moment, and I'll write up a receipt and get your change."

"I'll take the receipt, but let's not figure the bill yet. I might not be done paying taxes."

Mr. Blevins frowned at that. "Will, I assumed you knew... um... you see..."

"Yeah, I know that carpetbagger stole our farm. I'm not looking to pay it off. What did he buy it for, anyway?"

"Eleven dollars."

"Eleven dollars?"

"Yes, sir. Eleven dollars and seven cents, if memory serves. And I believe it does serve. Because every time one of these Yankee snakes comes in here and buys out a family farm, it burns me like a red-hot brand. It was eleven dollars, seven cents. I'd stake my life on it."

Will just stood there for a second, chewing on that. Eleven dollars and seven cents. His daddy had built that farm from nothing. Will had been born there, along with Rose, and two siblings who hadn't made it and who now lay beside Daddy near the creek beneath tiny headstones.

Will had spent his whole life there up till the war, and from the age of nine, he'd been the man of the place, plowing and planting, growing and working, keeping the place running, fixing it up, improving things.

And now it was gone.

For eleven dollars and seven cents.

Realizing he'd been standing there brooding for a while, he said abruptly, "How about the Kitner place?"

"What about it?" Mr. Blevins asked.

"Any carpetbagger snatch it up yet?"

"No sir."

"But it's on the market?"

"Yessir, on account of back taxes, like almost every other place in the county. Except for the plantations and the ones the carpetbaggers already got. Burns me, them coming in here and—"

"How much?" Will asked.

"How much what?" Mr. Blevins asked.

"How much for the Kitner place?"

"Oh, let me see." He flipped a few pages in his book then leaned close and looked over his glasses at the number beneath which he ran his finger. "Mr. Kitner had a little over two full sections and some nice improvements on that ground. He owed back taxes totaling forty-four dollars and eighty-seven cents."

"I'll take it," Will said.

Beside him, Maggie gasped.

He turned and smiled at her. "What? You told me to buy it for you."

"I wasn't serious. Will, that's a lot of money. You can't—"

"I just did. If I pay off those taxes, the property's mine, correct Mr. Blevins?"

Mr. Blevins frowned. "Well… yes. But… I hate to say this, Will…"

"What is it?"

"Well, you having worn the gray and all, you should know,

the Reconstructionists are confiscating the properties of ex-Confederates."

Will smiled. "Well, that won't be a problem at all, Mr. Blevins."

"I hate to be the bearer of bad tidings, Will, but things have changed here. I'm afraid it will be a problem. The bluebellies have a list of everyone who wore the gray. If you buy the Kitner place, there's sure to be the worst kind of trouble."

Will counted out the money and pushed it forward. "No sir, there won't be trouble. Because I'm not buying the Kitner place. Miss Dunne is."

CHAPTER 15

Will drove from the hardware store to Pelton's General Store and parked in the alley. Lumber, nails, whitewash, feed, and seed filled most of the wagon bed.

He didn't expect anyone to bother his stuff during the short time he'd be inside Pelton's, especially not with the bluebellies out in force today, but he didn't like taking stupid chances, so he hid his tool purchases under feed sacks.

Beside him, Maggie still sat there with the same expression she'd worn since leaving the county office: a dreamy smile and faraway eyes, as if she were happily dazed.

At least she'd finally stopped thanking him. For a while there, it looked like she never would.

"I just can't believe it's real," she said, as he helped her down from the wagon. "I mean… it's a dream come true."

"It's real, all right. Now, come on. Let's go inside and get what we need and get back out here before somebody decides to steal our stuff."

THE PROVIDER

"Oh, that would be terrible."

"It would. Let's go."

Will held the door for Maggie, and they went inside, where Mr. Pelton once again greeted them warmly.

This time, they really loaded up. Will hated to spend the money, but this was exactly why he'd worked so hard in Colorado, and why he'd gone without and saved his pennies: to provide for his family.

There would be much work to do at the new place. Things to clean and fix. Fields to plow and plant. Livestock to gather. They would need chickens and pigs and a milk cow first.

So he was in no hurry to return to town. Especially not with bluebellies prowling the streets. The very sight of them made him hear trumpets and smell gun smoke.

So he filled the rest of the wagon with bacon, eggs, butter, lard, corn meal, sausages, beans, cheese, salted pork, smoked hams, dried cod fish, pickled mackerel, sugar, molasses, maple syrup, soap, a gallon of coal oil, bedding, rice, three bushels of potatoes, a barrel of flour, more tea for Mama, and, for Maggie, some sour pickles.

"Don't go falling in the barrel now," he joked.

Maggie finally snapped out of her daze and made a face. "I won't, thank you very much. I learned my lesson."

"Your papa sure was angry that day," Mr. Pelton laughed.

"Yes, sir, he was. On rainy days, I still can't sit quite straight," she joked.

Will examined Pelton's guns. He wanted the ladies to be better armed, so he purchased all three derringers in stock: a pair of .41 caliber Remingtons and a four-barreled, .32 caliber Sharps pepperbox with a birdshead grip.

Figuring he should have a shotgun of his own, he also purchased a cut down, double-barrel, 10-gauge, Wm. Moore Company messenger gun, along with a bandolier that would hold fifty shells.

Mr. Pelton added these firearms and ammunition to Will's bill and announced the total, less apologetically this time, the man obviously happy to be back in business. "One hundred, sixty-one dollars and twenty-seven cents."

Maggie gulped and looked like she'd swallowed a peach pit. "That's a lot of money, Will."

"It is, but that's all right. This'll set us up for a while. Besides, we have enough money. This is exactly what I was saving for. So don't worry about it."

She clasped his hand. "This is so kind of you, Will. I don't know how to—"

"And please," Will interrupted, "don't set to thanking me again. I'm worn out with your gratitude. Let's get this stuff loaded up."

When they came out of the store, Will felt a prickle of apprehension. A second later, he knew why.

Across the street, just to one side of the sheriff's office, a small boy was pointing directly at him.

Beside the boy stood someone Will had totally and blissfully forgotten, a man he had once hated, a man he wished he never would have seen again.

Maggie, always attuned to Will's manner, read his expression and followed his gaze to where the tall, broad-shouldered man was grinning and starting across the street. "Who's that?" she asked.

"Roy Gibbs. Used to be an overseer at Weatherspoon's plantation. Real mean fella, real rough. Used to beat the tar out of us kids picking cotton."

"Is he the one who used to give you black eyes?"

Will nodded, watching the man approach, a familiar grin on his face.

It was the grin Gibbs showed people before he hurt them.

CHAPTER 16

Will had hated every second of picking cotton alongside the Weatherspoons' slaves. He worked the fields from dawn to dark, lugging fifty or sixty pounds behind him with the sun beating down. It was backbreaking work. The spiny cotton burrs made his hands a bloody mess. And yes, some nights, he also carted home a black eye from Roy Gibbs.

It was miserable, but that time of year it had been the only work that paid anything, so he had suffered through it year after year, every picking until he was seventeen and got into the big blowup that changed everything and brought an abrupt close to his cotton-picking career.

When Will was a boy, Gibbs had seemed impossibly huge and strong, a giant of a man straight out of a fairy tale.

Will set the flour barrel in the wagon and turned to face Gibbs, who came straight at him.

The man no longer looked impossibly huge. He was a couple of inches taller than Will but wiry, like a half-starved wolf. He had long arms and big hands, their knobby knuckles crisscrossed with scars from fighting. His black hair was streaked in gray now. Salt-and-pepper stubble bristled on his big, lantern jaw. His dark eyes glimmered, staring at Will, and he wore the same old, cruel and cocky smile on his face.

"Will Bentley," Gibbs said.

He stopped a few feet away, that stupid smile locked on his face.

Neither man offered to shake hands.

"What do you want, Gibbs?"

Gibbs ran his tongue in a slow circle around the inside of his cheek, saying nothing and staring at Will, obviously trying to intimidate him.

"I'm not a little kid anymore, Gibbs. You got something to say, say it."

But Gibbs continued to take his time, enjoying the moment, the man clearly feeling he was in control.

And Will remembered that about Gibbs now, remembered how everything had been a show with him. It wasn't enough to oversee slaves and kids who hired on to work alongside them. Wasn't even enough to beat them. Everything had to be a show. And Gibbs was its only star.

The memory rankled Will. He himself was a professional fighting man, not someone who looked for trouble, and he felt contempt for bullies like Gibbs.

"You going somewhere, Bentley?" Gibbs asked.

"That's none of your business," Will said. He wanted to load his wagon and leave, but he knew better than to pick up anything until Gibbs was gone.

He'd probably clock Will as soon as he picked up a bushel of potatoes.

"None of my business, huh?" Gibbs said. Then he turned his smile on Maggie and looked her up and down, his eyes glowing lecherously. "What do you think about that, darling?"

Will stepped in front of Maggie. "Don't talk to her, Gibbs. Don't even look at her."

Gibbs snorted. "Well, you sure have changed since you were a kid. You didn't make a peep out there in them cotton fields. You never got mouthy back then, even when I had to go upside your head."

Will balled his hands into fists. "Get out of here, Gibbs."

"Now, ain't that funny? Because I was gonna tell you the same thing. Get out of here, Bentley. Go back to wherever you've been and don't come back. Sully Weatherspoon doesn't want to see your face ever again."

Will smiled wolfishly. Now, he understood. Sully had sent Gibbs. Now it all made sense. Gibbs was still working for the Weatherspoons. "Sully doesn't want me around, huh? Must be afraid."

"You're lucky I wasn't there that day," Gibbs said.

"Is that so?" Will said and let his smile die. "Why's that?"

"Because I would've put you in your place. I would've beaten you to a pulp."

"Why don't you go ahead and pretend you were there that day? Go ahead and show me what you would've done. But watch out, Gibbs. I'm not a little kid anymore."

"I'm gonna bust your jaw," Gibbs said, and slipped his right hand into his pocket.

Will stepped to his own right, away from that hand and

whatever Gibbs was fixing to pull out of his pocket. But he didn't move too far, because if it was a gun, he didn't want to give Gibbs the room to move it.

Will brushed Maggie to safety behind him just as Gibbs brought his hand out again, the big fist gleaming with brass knuckles.

"Last chance, Bentley," Gibbs sneered. "Clear out of town for good or take your lumps."

That phrase—*take your lumps*—dredged up another bitter memory. Gibbs had always used that same phrase out in the fields, telling the children to take their lumps just before he beat them mercilessly.

Will crouched and raised his fists, ready.

Gibbs rushed forward and swung the brass knuckles at Will's face. There was no feint, no finesse; and Will's racing mind was not surprised.

Gibbs was a man accustomed to beating slaves and children, a man who had lumbered through life, hurting people, triumphing through size and brute strength and other edges, like a riding crop or whip or brass knuckles.

But those brass knuckles didn't do Gibbs a lick of good, because Will dipped the punch with ease and slammed his own fist into Gibbs's big jaw.

Gibbs staggered backward out of the alley to where a group of people had stopped to watch the unfolding drama.

Eyes blazing with fury, Gibbs charged and threw another right.

Will was ready for it. He stepped to one side, batted the punch away, and stepped back in with another cross that hammered home, flattening Gibbs's nose and sending him reeling again.

This time, Will followed, smashing Gibbs with slashing lefts and rights, making his big head jerk from side to side and snap backward from the force of the blows, which Will kept raining down, pounding and pounding, driving his former bully backward, out of the alley, into the street, striking the man's face with blow after thunderous blow, shifting his weight and putting every ounce of his tremendous strength into every shot.

Gibbs never recovered, never regained his balance, and never had a chance to throw another punch.

As Will had intended. Because war had taught him to strike fast and hard, and if you felt the enemy weaken, you hit them with everything you had until it was over.

Gibbs spilled into the street, totally unconscious, his face a bloody mess, his features rearranged in a mask of utter defeat.

"He started this," Will panted to those in attendance, and saw them staring at him with wonder and fear.

Then Maggie was beside him. "Are you all right, Will?"

"I'm fine." He crouched down and pulled the brass knuckles from the unconscious man's hand. "He does not need these."

Onlookers broke out of their paralysis then. A few scurried down the street, but most lingered, laughing and clapping Will on the shoulder.

"That'll make the saloon a lot nicer place for a while," one man said. "Gibbs comes in there every day at three with that Sully Weatherspoon, and everybody's gotta clear out or risk taking a beating."

"Yeah, thanks, Will," a vaguely familiar younger man said, clapping him on the back. "We owe you one."

"It was my pleasure," Will said, "but if you boys are feeling grateful, I'd appreciate your help loading this wagon. My hands are starting to hurt."

CHAPTER 17

Will's hands were battered and bruised but not broken. And praise God for that because he had a lot of work to do.

Riding out of town, he watched to make sure they weren't followed. They weren't.

That was good, but it was only a temporary reprieve. He had made quite a stir since coming back to Texas, not even counting the pair of bandits he'd shot dead along the way.

He had rescued Rose, humiliating Pew in the process, twisted his ear, and thrashed his hired man. He had called Sheriff Rickert's bluff and brazenly ignored his command to stay away from Pew.

Now, he'd beaten Gibbs unconscious, sending a message to his old enemy, Sully Weatherspoon, who was probably right in with the Reconstructionists. And from Will's understanding, that meant Sully might be able to sic the bluebellies on him.

So yes, trouble was coming. Likely big trouble. Might could even be shooting trouble.

But Will was not afraid. He was a Texan, after all, and Texans were born to trouble. After four years of war, he saw life as a sequence of violent clashes with periods of relative calm in between where you rested and worked and prepared for the inevitable hard times bound to come again and usually soon.

So while Will understood that forces would move against him, he would lose no sleep over this fact.

Still, he was glad he'd bought the extra weapons and ammunition.

"Mama and Rose are going to be so happy," Maggie said as they neared the farm.

"Seems like it. We got plenty of grub."

"And a new house," she said with a smile. "Don't forget that."

"Oh yeah, we got a house, too, didn't we?" Will joked.

"Seems strange, doesn't it? I mean buying the Kitner place?"

"I wouldn't have done it if Kitner was still there. Or even if I thought he was coming back."

"I know that," Maggie said. "What about the squatter?"

"He might be gone already. And if not, he'll figure out soon that the property is now occupied. I'm not worried about him."

"You don't worry much, do you?"

"No, ma'am, I don't. Never saw any percentage in worrying."

"Must be nice. I can't help but worry. But you want to know something funny? When you're around, I hardly worry. Even when that terrible Mr. Gibbs pulled out those… what are they called again?"

"Brass knuckles," Will said, slapping the pocket where they now rode.

"Right. Even when he pulled out those brass knuckles, I felt utterly calm. I knew that you would whup him. Do you think he'll be okay?"

Will shrugged. "Don't know, don't care. Gibbs started it. And he tried to hit me with brass knuckles. They are a lethal weapon. He bought his own fate."

"Well, I hope he doesn't die."

"It was self-defense. And I have plenty of witnesses who'll testify to that."

"None of that will matter if Sully Weatherspoon sets the bluebellies on you."

"Yeah, well, we'll see. Like I said, I'm not worried about it."

"Where are you going?" Maggie asked when he passed the turn to her place.

"To the new house, of course."

"What about Mama and Rose?"

"We'll fetch them soon enough. But I'd like to have another look before you women fill the house with chatter."

Maggie laughed. "All right, Mr. Bentley. We'll have a look. That'll give me a chance to at least sweep the kitchen and put away some of the groceries before they come. It'll be nice to welcome them into a tidy, well-stocked kitchen."

They came down the main trail, which was still free of tracks.

Will parked in back, near the kitchen, and got down and checked for signs of the squatter.

"He was here again," Will said, pointing out the new tracks and fresh horse droppings.

Maggie's eyes swelled. "Is it safe?"

"Yeah, he's gone. Must have come back while we were away,

THE PROVIDER

seen we'd been around, and ridden off again. We probably won't see him again."

"But what if..." she started and then chuckled to herself, shaking her head. "Don't worry about it, right?"

"Right."

"What should we unload first?"

"Let's take another look first, then unload everything."

She smiled with excitement. "All right, Will. That sounds good. This is fun. I can't believe it's even true."

"It's true," Will said. He opened the door and held it for her and gestured her inside. "Your new home, Miss Dunne."

Maggie stepped inside, studying the kitchen with glittering eyes. "Not my house. Yours. It was your money, Will."

Will shook his head. "It's not mine. Look at the deed. It's your name on there. This is your home and your ranch."

"My name might be on the deed, but you know what I mean. You bought it. You own it. It's your home."

Will stared into her eyes. "How about we make it *our* home?"

She stared back at him, eyes glistening with emotion. "You have no idea how good that sounds to me."

"Me, too. I love the idea of sharing a home with you."

She stepped closer and stared up at him. "Are you serious, Will?"

"I am."

"And you don't mean as a sister, do you?"

"I do not."

"Oh, Will," she said and gave a strange, short laugh, and then she was wiping at the corners of her eyes. "I'm so happy I could kiss you."

"Don't tease me like that, Maggie."

She lifted her chin a little, staring boldly into his eyes. "I'm not teasing. I've never kissed a man before. Or even a boy for that matter. But I'm not teasing, not one little bit, Will Bentley. I could kiss you right now."

Will reached out and took her pretty face in his hands and lowered his mouth to hers and they kissed softly, broke apart, looked into each other's eyes, then kissed again, long and deeply.

Finally, they just stood there, holding each other, both of them very happy and excited and boiling over with optimism.

"If I tell you something," Will said, "do you promise not to laugh at me?"

"No. But tell me anyway."

"That was my first time, too."

Maggie's mouth dropped wide open. "That was your first time kissing a girl?"

He nodded, and they both burst out in happy laughter, still clinging to each other.

"Will?"

"Yeah?"

"Would you kiss me again?"

"I'd love to."

"Do it, then."

"Not yet. I gotta say something first."

She smirked at him. "Now who's filling up the house with chatter?"

He laughed. "Well, you got me there, but this is important. I know this is kind of sudden, Maggie, but I like you an awful lot."

"I like you, too, Will. An awful lot. I always have. But now more than ever. Way more."

He took her face in his hands again and stared into her shimmering green eyes. "Maggie, what I'm trying to say is… I mean, what I want to ask…"

She blinked up at him expectantly, her smile growing wider.

"Will you marry me?" he asked.

"Oh Will!" she cried. "Yes, I would love to marry you!"

CHAPTER 18

~~~

Will unloaded everything while Maggie swept and dusted the kitchen.

It took them a while, because, having both kissed for the first time, they kept stopping to try it again. And again. And again.

Finally, when the supplies were put away and the kitchen was tidied, they rode next door to share the good news.

The whole ride over, Maggie leaned against Will, that same, happy, half-stunned look on her face.

When they pulled up to the bunkhouse, she asked him to kiss her again.

She didn't have to ask twice.

Then she said, "You're serious, right? You really want to marry me?"

"Maggie, how long have you known me?"

"My whole life."

"So do you think I'd ask you to marry me if I didn't mean it?"

"No," she said, and smiled. "I shouldn't even have asked. It's just... I'm so happy, I can't believe it. After my family died, I thought I'd never be happy again. But now... oh, Will, I'm so very happy."

"So am I, Maggie. I didn't know I could be this happy."

They kissed again then composed themselves and went inside.

As soon as Rose saw Maggie's face, she shot up from the chair where she'd been sewing and said, "He asked you, didn't he?"

At the far end of the table, Mama smiled, her eyes twinkling.

Maggie, who had apparently already discussed the possibility of marriage, nodded.

Rose gave a happy cry and ran to her best friend, and they hugged and laughed and set to crying.

Women, Will thought, *what strange and wonderful creatures.*

Mama caught Will's eye and smiled, nodding, letting him know she approved of the union. Then, after giving the two girls a moment, she rose and went to Maggie and embraced her and said, "I couldn't be happier—or prouder—to call you my daughter, Maggie. May God bless you both."

"Oh, thank you, Mama," Maggie said, hugging Mama tight.

Will stood there with his hat in his hands, feeling a little out of place.

Then the women turned on him and pretty near hugged the stuffing out of him.

After that, the women were all talking at the same time.

Will nudged Maggie. "Let's take them next door."

"Next door?" Rose said.

"Oh!" Maggie said. "We forgot to tell you. Will bought the Kitner place."

This kicked off another happy round of questions and hugging.

After that, they gathered their things from the bunkhouse and put them in the wagon and got the horses and Will's mules and tethered the mules to the wagon and headed next door, with Mama and Rose driving the wagon and Will and Maggie on horseback.

They left a good deal of stuff in the stable, things Mama and Rose had saved from the farm when they were kicked out. It would be easy enough to come back later and get it all.

At the new house, the women went from room to room, looking everything over and chattering with delight and talking excitedly about where everything would go and all the work that needed done.

Will left them to it and went outside and took care of the animals then started unloading the wagon. His hands hurt from the fight. They were bruised and swollen, but they worked all right, and that's what mattered. Usually, as long as you don't punch somebody high up or in the back of the skull, you were all right.

Of course, hitting them in the teeth isn't so great, either, he thought, examining his lacerated knuckles.

Oh well. He'd heal.

Things were good now. Better than good. Better than he could have ever imagined.

Yes, Texas was still a mess. Yes, he had a heap of trouble coming his way. Yes, there was a bunch of work to do. And yes, his hands were all cut up, but he and Maggie now owned this ranch, and they were going to be married and start a life together.

He just had to work hard and stay alert and wait for Texas to rise again. And, he thought, staring out across the creek toward his former family farm, someday, he would get the old homeplace back, and then he and Maggie would own it, this place, and her old place, which amounted, all in, to over two thousand well-watered acres with plenty of grass.

As he'd told Maggie, they needed pigs and chickens and a milk cow. With those things, crops, a good rifle, and plenty of ammo, a family could get by.

But Will wanted to do more than merely survive. He wanted to provide for his family and provide amply, wanted to—

His thoughts broke off abruptly when he saw the lone, dark rider cutting across the field, coming this way.

The squatter was coming back.

CHAPTER 19

The rider lifted a hand in the air.

Will waved back, and the man kept coming.

He was a small, tough-looking black man riding a small, tough-looking bay.

"Howdy," the man said, drawing rein a short distance away.

"Howdy," Will said. The man was young and looked vaguely familiar. "You the one who's been staying here?"

"Yessir," the man said, studying Will in a way that made Will think the man half-recognized him, too. "You moving in?"

Will nodded. "Just bought the place."

"All right," the man said. Disappointment showed on his gaunt face. These were hard times, and Will knew they were extra hard on recently freed slaves, who were trying to make their way in a strange, new world that could turn violent at the drop of a hat. "I'll move along then."

"You look like you could use a meal," Will said. "Why don't

climb down, and I'll get you something to eat. Your horse looks like he could use some grain, too."

"Thank you, mister. Trouble is, I ain't got no money."

"I'm giving, not selling."

"Well, thank you very much," the man said. "You need any help? I'd be happy to give you a hand unloading that wagon. It'd make me feel better about eating your grub."

"That works," Will said.

The man climbed down, studying him again.

Will stuck out his hand. "Welcome. I'm—"

"Will Bentley?" the man asked, shaking his hand.

"That's right. I'm sorry, friend. You look familiar to me, but I can't remember how I know you."

"My name's Rufus Twill," the man said, and a huge smile spread across his face. "I didn't recognize you at first because you're a lot bigger than you were back then."

"Back when, Mr. Twill?"

"You saved my hide, maybe even saved my life."

"I did?"

"Oh yeah. Sully would've killed me for dropping that dresser and cracking the mirror."

Now, it was Will's turn to smile. "Mouse?"

"That's right. But I go by Rufus now, not Mouse."

Will laughed and clapped him on the shoulder. "I'm not the only one who put on size. You're a lot bigger than you were."

"I was just a kid back then, Mr. Bentley. Probably twelve years old. I'm eighteen now."

"It's good to see you, Rufus," Will said, "and call me Will. Take care of your horse. There's grain just inside the door. Then I'll introduce you to my family and... my fiancé."

It was strange—and strangely thrilling—referring to Maggie that way.

Rufus thanked him, but before he could see to the bay, the door opened, and Mama, Rose, and Maggie came outside.

"Rufus," Will said, "meet my mama, Mrs. Bentley; my sister, Rose; and my fiancé, Maggie Dunne."

Rufus swept the hat from his head and gave a little bow to each of the women.

"This is Rufus Twill," Will said.

The women all said it was nice to meet Rufus, who smiled back at them. "It's nice to meet you ladies."

"Rufus and I knew each other back before the war. We picked cotton together."

"And Will saved my hide," Rufus said.

"How?" Maggie asked.

"We were out there, working in the hot sun, and my owner's son, Sully, came riding out and told Will and me to come with him because he had some work for us at the house."

"Sully Weatherspoon?" Maggie asked.

"Yes, ma'am."

"Of all the men to work for…"

"Yes, ma'am, he was a tough one."

"He was," Will agreed, remembering that day. "But I was happy when he told us to go to the house, because it gave me a chance to straighten my back and leave that cotton sack behind for a while."

"Backbreaking work," Rufus said. "That's the one thing I won't ever do again. No, sir. It's no use being free if I gotta pick cotton. I'd sooner starve."

"I don't blame you," Will said. Then to the women, he said,

"Ended up being worse at the house than out in the field, though."

"Oh," Rose said, putting two and two together. "You're the one who dropped the dresser?"

Rufus smiled sheepishly. "Yes, ma'am. That was me. I wasn't very big at the time, and my hands were slick with sweat, and the dresser was heavy."

"Wait, I've never heard this story," Maggie said. "What dresser?"

"Sully had bought this big old dresser in town," Will said. "It was sitting there in the back of the wagon, and he told us to carry it inside. I asked if maybe we ought to get a couple more people to help, but that just made him mad. He told me to move it or he'd fire me. We needed the money."

Mama frowned. "I remember this story now."

"We were carrying it in, and my end slipped," Rufus explained, "and the mirror on top broke."

"It was loud," Will said. "Sully came running out of the house, shouting with a riding crop in one hand. I had never seen anybody so mad in all my life."

"Then, when Sully started asking what happened, Will said he had dropped the thing, not me."

Will shrugged. "I knew what Sully did to his slaves. But all he could to me was fire me. Or so I thought."

"Sully started cursing out Will and hit him with his riding crop, and then..." Rufus grinned.

"I warned him," Will said.

"What happened?" Maggie wanted to know.

"I warned him not to hit me again, but he slashed that crop right across the side of my head. So I punched him."

"Broke his nose and knocked him out cold," Rufus laughed. "I lit out of there like my tail was on fire. That was the last time I ever saw Will."

"Is that what Gibbs meant?" Maggie asked Will. "When he said he wished he'd been there that day?"

Will nodded. "That's what he meant."

"You run into Gibbs?" Rufus said, looking half-sick at the mention of the overseer's name.

"You could say that."

"More like Gibbs ran into Will," Maggie said. "And specifically, Will's fist. A whole bunch of times."

"You scrapped with Gibbs?"

Will nodded and held out his bruised hands. "Just this morning."

"Your hands are banged up, but your face looks all right," Rufus said, a grin coming onto his face. "You whup him?"

"Will crushed him," Maggie said. "And Gibbs had brass knuckles."

Then, with great enthusiasm, Maggie told the story of the fight, finishing with, "He asked for it, and Will gave it to him."

Rufus slapped his thighs. "I wish I had seen it! That man beat me a hundred times. Once, I thought I was gonna lose my eye." But then he grew suddenly serious. "Sully won't let that stand."

"Probably not," Will said. "But we'll see. After I knocked him out, I remember sitting at home, waiting for the sheriff to come, but he never did."

"Sully was too embarrassed to tell anyone what happened, I'll bet," Rose said.

"Either that or Mr. Weatherspoon didn't want it to get out,"

Rufus said. "Mr. Weatherspoon was awful careful about the family name. I hope Sully leaves you alone again this time."

"We'll see," Will said again. "I'm not worried about it. Why don't you go ahead and take care of your horse. Then we'll get you some food. And afterward, you can help me unload this stuff."

"Much obliged," Rufus said. "Truth be told, I haven't had a meal in a long time."

"You handy?" Will asked.

"Sure am," Rufus said proudly. "What I want to do is run cattle, but I can do pretty much anything… other than pick cotton, that is."

"Well, if you want to stick around for a while, I got a lot of work to do. If you'll help me, we'll feed you, and I'll pay you a dollar a day."

Rufus's eyes lit up. "A dollar a day?"

"And three square meals," Will said. "You can sleep in the bunkhouse and feed your horse out of my grain."

"How long do I have to work here?"

"We'll take it day by day. You want to leave, leave. You're a free man now."

"Yessir, I am," a smiling Rufus said, sticking his hand out again. "Thank you, Will. You got yourself a deal."

CHAPTER 20

That evening, after a big supper, Will asked Maggie if she would take a stroll with him.

Rufus, who'd worked hard alongside Will all afternoon then enjoyed the meal with the family, excused himself and headed for the bunkhouse, thanking them all again and wishing them a good night.

"Are you courting me now, Mr. Bentley?" Maggie asked when they were alone outside.

He pulled her into his arms, and they kissed for a long time.

When they stepped apart again, Will said, "I've been wanting to do that all day long."

"Me, too," Maggie said. "I'm so happy, Will. I just can't believe this is true."

"Believe it."

They started walking again, holding hands now.

"God has blessed us beyond measure," Maggie said.

"He has. But we have a lot of work to do."

"Rufus seems like a good worker."

"He is a good worker. I'm bullheaded enough to tackle a heap of work on my lonesome, but I sure am glad to have him here. We're late getting stuff in the ground. We gotta plow and plant."

"You don't think we're too late, do you?"

"No ma'am, I do not. I have to say, I think everything's gonna work out fine. Just fine."

"Will Bentley, I don't remember you being such an optimist when we were children."

"I didn't have time for optimism."

"What does that mean?" she laughed.

"I don't know," he confessed with a chuckle of his own. "Just seemed like the thing to say. Guess you bring out the optimist in me."

"I could say the same thing about you. Suddenly, I feel like anything is possible."

They walked along through the gathering gloom, following a beaten path toward the creek.

"So," Maggie said finally, "how long are you going to make me wait?"

"Wait for what?"

"To get married."

"Oh."

"I hope you're not looking to drag out our engagement."

"Not at all."

"So when do you want to get married?"

"How does tomorrow sound?"

Her eyes bulged. "Tomorrow?"

"We can wait."

"No... I was just... surprised was all." She laughed. "Tomorrow would be wonderful."

They embraced and kissed again.

"Will?"

"Yeah?"

"How do we get married?"

"I don't even know. We'll need a preacher."

"What about Andrew McLean just down the road?"

Will chuckled. "Andrew's a little crazy, but sure. If he'll marry us, that'll work."

"And then, don't we have to get a marriage license or something?"

"If it's important to you, we can get a license," Will said, "but a piece of paper doesn't matter to me. This is between you, me, and God, not the law. The less folks in town know about us, the safer you are."

Maggie smiled up at him. "I don't care about those people or the law or any piece of paper. I only care about marrying you."

"Then tomorrow morning, I'll put on my new duds, and we'll go see Andrew McLean."

While Will was working with Rufus that day, the women had made him a new shirt and pants. It was just a simple set of clothes, but he sure was happy to have them after spending so much time in his raggedy old duds.

Maggie glanced down and frowned at herself. "I wish I had time to make a new dress. This is my nicest one, and it's worn out."

"You look beautiful," he said, meaning it.

"Thank you, Will, but a woman wants to look nice for her wedding day."

"We can wait if you want time to get material and make a dress," Will said.

"Not on your life," Maggie said. "I wish we could go get married right now."

"So do I. You could always go to town and buy a dress."

"A store-bought dress? Will Bentley, are you trying to spoil me?"

"If ever a girl deserved spoiling, it's you."

"Well, I appreciate the offer, but no thank you. You should save your money. I don't need a fancy dress. In fact, I don't even need to make a new dress. I just need you."

"That suits me just fine," Will said, secretly relieved. It would be a good idea to avoid town for a while. "Tomorrow morning, we'll go get married, and you'll make me the happiest man in Texas."

"You've already made me the happiest woman alive," Maggie said, coming into his arms. "Now make me even happier and kiss me again."

He was happy to oblige.

THEY WERE MARRIED THE NEXT MORNING IN AN IMPROMPTU ceremony behind Andrew McLean's rickety shack. Will wore his new shirt and pants, and Maggie looked absolutely stunning in her normal blue dress.

Andrew McLean, who'd been feeding the hogs when they'd pulled up, wore his filthy clothes but did wash his hands thoroughly before fetching the Bible and coming back outside.

It was a brief ceremony befitting a brief courtship. McLean

spoke a bit about love and marriage but thankfully didn't launch into one of his fire and brimstone sermons.

Will and Maggie said the words, McLean pronounced them man and wife, and they kissed before the smiling attendees: Mama, Rose, Rufus, and Andrew McLean's wife, Katrina, a dark-haired Swiss German who pulled out a dusty accordion and played "The Yellow Rose of Texas," singing in a reckless warble that made Will twitch a little.

Despite the preacher in his filthy shirt and Katrina McLean's awful singing, Will had never been happier.

In just three days, he had come home, bought a ranch, recognized his perfect match, and made her his wife.

Life could not get any better than this.

CHAPTER 21

The next two weeks were the happiest Will had ever known.

He and Rufus plowed and planted and repaired the house and outbuildings, which had been abandoned for some time. The women cleaned the house and stable, helped with the planting, and saw to the cooking and laundry and the making and mending of clothes.

The days were long and busy and happy.

For Will and Maggie, their nights alone were even happier.

When Will and Rufus worked together, they talked. Rufus did most of the talking, and what he talked of was freedom.

Many former slaves were still trapped in their old lives, free in words only. But Rufus was determined to live free or die, and Will reckoned they saw eye to eye on that.

Ironically, defending freedom had led Will to join the Confederacy; but only through their defeat had Rufus gained his freedom.

Such paradoxes sometimes occurred to Will. He didn't waste time pondering them, instead chalking them up to God working in mysterious ways, a thing every soldier knew.

"I'd sooner die than go back to the Weatherspoons," Rufus said.

Will nodded. He could understand that.

"You know what I really want to do, though?" Rufus asked.

"Tell me."

"I want to gather cattle and drive them to market."

"I heard folks are making money doing that."

"Yessir, that's a fact. It's hard work. Dangerous. But I got a knack with cattle. Mr. Weatherspoon was one of the only men who managed to hold a herd through the war. I got out of the fields at fourteen and worked with the cattle. The last couple of years, I was foreman. Even went on a few gathers after the army confiscated some of Mr. Weatherspoon's cattle. Rode down into the Thicket."

"Rough country. I had an uncle who lived down there. Used to visit him from time to time, but he died in the war."

Rufus nodded. "Yeah, it's rough all right. Dangerous. Cattle down there are wild and crafty. Some of them old mossyhorns are meaner than wild boars. Some of them'll catch a man's scent and hunt him like prey."

"Guess you want to be loaded for bear."

"You got that right. It ain't just the bulls that'll trouble you. You gotta look out all the time. The Thicket's got snakes and quicksand and tall-growing thorns that'll put out your eyes, you make one wrong turn working the brakes."

"These days, the biggest threat is men like Teal and his gang.

They're hiding out down there. I wouldn't want to go down and run into that bunch," Will said.

Of course, that was only half true. He very much wanted to run into Teal, very much wanted to make him pay for what he'd done to Maggie's family and other Texans and for robbing the bank that held all Will's money.

But a fight like that, he would need it to be on his terms, not Teal's. Teal was a fighting man, a ruthless marauder who rode at the front of a gang of murdering savages, every last one of them battle-tested and hard as nails.

"That Thicket's so big, you'd have to have awful bad luck to run into Teal or his kind," Rufus said. "But yeah, you'd want to be careful. They like nothing better than stringing up black men—or people like you, folks who give us a chance."

"Lot riskier than raising corn."

Rufus shrugged. "I'm learning risk is what makes life worth living."

Will couldn't disagree. Unless you were born into wealth, like Sully Weatherspoon, you needed to work hard and take risks to build a good life.

"Men are making big money on cattle these days," Rufus said. "They've been running herds to Kansas and Louisiana, and now, the north and west are opening up. Colorado, Wyoming, even."

"I heard about that," Will said. "Heard Charles Goodnight just struck a deal with the railroad up in Cheyenne."

Rufus nodded. "Heard that, too."

"Long way to drive cattle."

"It is. But it can be done. Men are getting rich."

"How rich?"

"I hear twenty dollars a head."

Will whistled. "That's a lot of money."

"Yessir, it surely is. If we could get some men and gather some longhorns down in the Thicket, we could get some of it for ourselves."

"Lot of risk," Will said.

"Yessir, and a lot of reward."

Will nodded. "You've captured my interest, Rufus."

"It'd only take us a week and a half to drive them to Fort Worth. Or, if we had enough men, we could head up the Chisholm Trail to Abilene."

"Long way."

"Around five hundred miles, I hear."

"Dangerous trip."

"For a war veteran, you seem awful concerned with danger."

"Veterans understand danger in a way most folks don't. All this money you're talking about isn't worth a thing if we get ourselves killed."

There was more to Will's reluctance than just danger, however. He was a newlywed and hated the idea of being separated from Maggie.

Besides, he still had money left.

Of course, that money would run out. He could get by without it, but once you've had money, you'll work extra hard and take on some risk to avoid going broke again.

He'd have to keep thinking about it.

"You have a point," Rufus said. "But like I said, we could sell them at Fort Worth. Not for twenty a head, but we would still make some money."

"Or tie in with somebody who knows the trail."

"Beef business is booming right now. And folks don't care if you're Union or Confederate, white or black, so long as you do the work. About the only other job like that is the railroad, and I'd rather drive cattle than lay track."

Will nodded. "Me, too. Even though I like building things."

"You're good at it."

Will held up his big hands. "God blessed me that way. I can build anything. But I think laying track would get monotonous after a while."

"And it's just as dangerous as driving cattle."

"Even worse from what I hear."

"Well, you think on it, Will. You want to throw in together, say the word, and we'll ride down into the Thicket and get us some cattle."

Will nodded again, warming to the idea. "I'd need a cattle horse."

"We'll find you a cattle horse. There are folks around here, used to run big herds, got them all snatched up and never rebuilt. One of them would sell you a horse. But if we're gonna do it, we gotta hurry. The cattle boom won't last forever. You got this much money changing hands, this many hungry people, you're gonna see everybody and his brother rounding up cattle. It'll get a lot harder to make a buck. Now's the time."

Will chuckled. "You're a persuasive fellow, Rufus."

Rufus spread his calloused hands. "It ain't me doing the persuading, it's the opportunity."

"Well, I'll think on it," Will said, and felt the seed of this idea already swelling in his mind.

He might even have kept talking about it more if a boy on a mule hadn't come riding into view then, shouting Will's name, his voice full of panic.

CHAPTER 22

It was Denny Smith, a boy from down the road, whose daddy, another veteran, had recently stopped for a visit one evening.

Will and Rufus walked out to meet him.

"Mr. Bentley!" Denny shouted as he drew close. "The law's hunting you, sir!"

"All right," Will said, and one hand dropped unconsciously to the Colt shoved through his belt. "Bluebellies or Rickert?"

"It's Sheriff Rickert, sir. He said you stirred up some trouble in town and he's gonna bring you to justice, sir."

"Oh yeah? Where is he?"

"Riding around, talking to folks, asking about you. Of course, nobody'll tell a thing, sir. Except maybe for…"

The boy nodded across the creek in the direction of Will's former home and the Yankee carpetbagger, Mr. Braintree.

Will hadn't talked to the man since their unpleasant introduction, but he'd seen Braintree puttering around the property and stared him down more than once.

A foolish thing to do, giving in to anger like that. He'd known it was a foolish thing when he'd done it, but he'd done it anyway out of spite. He didn't like the man and would get his property back someday.

But Denny was right. Braintree would give him up in a heartbeat.

"All right, Denny, I appreciate you riding all the way over here to warn me. And for riding in a hurry."

The boy stood up a little straighter. "Yes, sir, Mr. Bentley. We're neighbors, sir. You can always count on us."

"Likewise," Will said and reached up to shake hands, which pleased the boy immensely.

"Where was Rickert last you knew?"

"Just leaving our place, sir. He was heading toward the Edsel farm."

"How many men in the posse?"

"Just Sheriff Rickert and two other men. I don't know their names."

"All right, son. I appreciate the warning."

He cut the kid loose and headed for the stable. Rufus stuck with him.

"I'd best ride over there and intercept the sheriff before he keeps poking around and figures out where I live," Will said.

He grabbed the mule saddle.

"Ain't you taking Honey?" Rufus asked.

"Nah, there could be trouble, and if Honey got hurt, I wouldn't want to face Mrs. Bentley."

Rufus grabbed his saddle. "Makes sense. Let's go, then."

"This is my trouble, not yours."

"If it's your trouble, Will, it's my trouble, too."

"I can handle it."

"I have no doubt. But I'm riding along anyway."

"Rickert won't like it."

"He doesn't have to like it."

Will chuckled. "All right, my friend. We'll ride together. I appreciate it."

Will fetched his Spencer, his new shotgun, and his bandolier of shells, briefly told the women what was happening, then grabbed Mama's shotgun and walked out.

There wasn't time for discussion. If Rickert found out where he lived, he'd tell Pew, and Pew might tell the Weatherspoons.

Outside, he handed the shotgun to Rufus.

"Ever shoot one of these?"

"No sir."

"Simplest thing in the world. Just cock the hammers, point it, and pull the trigger. You want to fire the other barrel, pull the second trigger."

"I can do that."

"It's got a kick to it, but there's no deadlier weapon up close. These buckshot shells each hold nine .32 caliber pellets. Inside of fifty feet, you can't miss."

Will handed him a few extra shells and taught him to break open the gun and reload.

"That's dead simple," Rufus said.

"Yessir, it is," Will said. "Better take this, too." He handed him the Dragoon.

Rufus accepted the revolver and shoved it naturally through his belt, making Will think he'd handled guns before.

"You know how to shoot that?" Will asked.

"Yessir. Used to carry one just like this down into the Thicket."

"You ever shoot anybody before?"

"No sir."

"Hopefully you won't have to today. But if you do, aim for the breastbone."

Rufus nodded solemnly, and they rode out.

It took them a while to locate the sheriff.

Rickert and the two men with him came riding out of the Grady place, about three miles from Will's ranch.

Will heard them before he saw them and whispered to Rufus to spread out to either side of the lane. By following their voices, he caught sight of them through the trees, riding this way.

He was sitting his mule with the shotgun across his saddle, thirty feet away, when Rickert and the other men came onto the main road.

Rickert was talking loudly about some catfish he'd caught and broke off with a curse when he saw Will sitting there.

All three men reined in, completely surprised.

"You men keep your hands off your weapons," Will said, "and I won't have to cut you down with this scattergun."

He hefted it in view without pointing it in their direction.

"Don't go waving that thing around," Rickert said.

One of the men with him, a blond-haired youth Will believed to be one of the Smith boys, nodded silently and kept his hands in plain view.

The other rider, a tough-looking man Will didn't recognize, said, "There's three of us and only one of him."

"This shotgun doesn't care," Will said. "You're feeling lucky, buddy, you just go ahead and grab iron. But I gotta warn you. You'll get the other two killed, too."

Rickert and the Smith kid edged away from the other man, who just scowled at Will.

"Besides," Rufus said from behind the men. "He ain't alone."

"What in tarnation?" Rickert said.

The Smith kid looked like he wanted to be somewhere else.

The tough guy cursed and said some nasty things about Rufus.

"You keep talking like that, I might just shoot you for the fun of it," Rufus said.

"Now, let's everybody just calm down," Rickert said. All the color had drained from his face. He'd never been much of a sheriff, but he knew enough, apparently, to understand he was a dead man if anything kicked off. Will and Rufus had flanked them at angles that wouldn't put each other in danger if they let fly with the buckshot.

"Heard you been hunting me," Will said.

"That's right," Rickert said. "I told you to leave Pew alone."

"Let me ask you something, Rickert," Will said. "If Pew kidnapped your sister, would you let him have her?"

"I don't have a sister."

"Your daughter, then."

Rickert frowned. "No, probably not. But I'd go through the law."

"That's what I tried to do," Will said. "Remember? You told me you couldn't help."

Rickert sputtered a little before changing tack. "Pew's

madder than a hornet. So I want you to come back with me, and we'll get this sorted out."

"There's nothing to sort out. Unless you're gonna charge Pew with kidnapping."

"Charge Pew?"

"That's right. If you charge Pew with kidnapping, I might come before the judge and give my testimony."

"Be reasonable, Will. You don't want trouble with the law."

"You're not riding for the law, Rickert. You're riding for Pew."

"You can't talk to me that way."

"I just did," Will said. Disgust was rising in him now. "You want to do something about it, Sheriff? You want to tell these other men to step aside, face me, man-to-man, right now?"

Rickert shook his head. "That's enough of that sort of talk. I am an officer of the law." He tapped the badge on his chest.

"That badge might mean something in town, Rickert, but out here, the only thing that matters is bullets... and buckshot." Will hoisted the shotgun again. "This is my jurisdiction. You don't come out here again unless you're invited."

"Where you living at, Bentley?" the tough guy asked.

Will swiveled his gaze onto the man. "What's your name?"

The man glared back at him. "My name's Butler. Chad Butler."

Will nodded. He'd heard of Butler. Had a reputation in town. Just after the war, he'd gotten into a fight at the saloon and shot a man.

"Well, Butler, I'll offer you the same chance I offered Rickert. We can throw down man-to-man, right now, just the two of us."

Butler thought about it. "Put down that scattergun, and I'll do it."

Will chuckled, shaking his head. "Not my fault you rode out here with a revolver. Seems like you boys underestimated me."

"I won't next time," Butler said.

"Next time, huh? Well, like I told Rickert. You boys best not come out here again uninvited. You do, I'll bury all three of you back in the pines."

"I never figured you for one of these rabble-rousing troublemakers, Will," Rickert said. "You're just like that swamp raider Teal."

"I'm nothing like Teal. I'm just a man who wants to be left alone. But if you push, I'll stir up trouble like you've never seen, like you've never even dreamed of. Folks around here know me. And they like me, Rickert, which is more than you can say. Folks are sick of you and the bluebellies and the carpetbaggers and all the bootlickers. Folks are primed for a fight. And they'll know I'm in the right. You push me, and I'll raise an army."

Rickert, clearly rattled by Will's threat, lifted his empty palms. "Nobody's pushing. You just calm down, and I'll tell Pew I couldn't find you. Ain't no call to go talking that way."

"My words stand," Will said.

Rickert shook his head and turned toward town. The other men followed. Butler looked back over his shoulder, letting Will know they weren't finished.

The pragmatic side of Will considered pulling the Spencer and knocking Butler out of his saddle, but that would be murder, so he figured he'd just bide his time and stay ready for Butler.

Rufus, sidling up next to Will, said, "Felt good, making them squirm."

"Yeah, well, I meant what I said. They come back, I'm done talking. And I figure at least Butler will be back at some point. I won't blame you if you want to ride out of here."

"Ride out of here?" Rufus said incredulously. "I haven't even finished talking you into gathering cattle yet. We're partners, Will. If those men come for you, they'll have to deal with me, too."

CHAPTER 23

Will propped up on an elbow and studied his beautiful young wife, who lay panting happily beside him, sparkling with perspiration in the candlelight.

"That sure did feel good, Mr. Bentley," she joked. "I'm not sure how I lived life without it."

"Well, I'm glad you waited for me."

"And I'm glad you waited for me, sir."

He leaned in and kissed her ear.

She flinched away, grinning. "Now, don't you go kissing my ear, or you'll just start things up again."

"Talk about an idle threat," Will said and went after her ear again.

She blocked him and sat up, lovely in the candlelight. "Just give me a second to catch my breath."

"All right."

"Will?"

"Yeah?"

"Are you worried?"

"About what?"

"Rickert."

"No. I already told you that."

"I know. But I am."

"Don't be."

She stood from the bed and paced back and forth, voicing her concerns.

Eventually, Will, who had been mesmerized by the sight of his lovely wife, realized she'd asked him something. "Huh?"

Maggie stopped pacing and stared down at him, hands on hips. "Weren't you listening to me?"

"Not really," he said. "I was distracted."

She smirked at him. "Well, close your eyes if you can't concentrate."

"Not on your life, Mrs. Bentley."

"Well, try harder then. Don't you think Rickert will be back?"

"I doubt it. I think I got through to him."

"You mean you scared him?"

"Yeah. Him and the kid. That other one, Chad Butler, he's a different story."

"You think he'll come back?"

"I think he'd like to. But will he come back on his own? I doubt it. And what's he going to do, stir folks up because I twisted Pew's ear and whipped Gibbs? People would run him out of town on a rail."

"Still, I don't trust these people. Pew, the Weatherspoons, you just never know what they'll do."

"You're right about that."

"So why aren't you worried?"

"First of all, I don't worry. I plan."

"You know what I mean, though, Will."

"I do. But it's an important distinction."

"All right."

"If there's a credible threat, you gotta prepare for it. Ignoring it would be stupid. Maybe even suicidal."

"You don't consider these people a credible threat?"

"Not the way I'm talking. Do I think they'll give up? Not yet. But I'm not worried about a bunch of them riding out here tomorrow. There would be no reason for it."

"You threatened an officer of the law."

"Even Rickert knew I was right about that."

"Yeah, well, still."

"Okay, still. Pew and the Weatherspoons are up in arms, but they have a lot to lose. They'll try to do things by the book."

"What if they send the bluebellies?"

"The bluebellies don't want to come out here. It'd be different if I stirred up real trouble. But nobody wants to die over the charges they could lodge against me. Besides, I made sure Rickert heard me loud and clear. They got a lot to lose by pushing me. If they label me a rabble-rouser, I'll rouse a rabble like they've never seen."

She looked at him. "You're a little scary."

"Scary?"

"Yeah, a little. When you talk like that, this light comes into your eyes."

"Well, don't you worry about it, Maggie. I am here to provide for you. And if you need me to provide protection, then yes, I will protect you, and that means doing whatever needs to be done, even... scary things."

"All right, Will," she said, crawling back into bed with him. "I just hope nothing comes of all this."

"Likewise. I don't want anything taking me away from my husbandly duties."

"Speaking of which, have you given any more thought to gathering cattle with Rufus?"

"I have. It's a good idea."

She frowned again. "It's a dangerous idea."

"A lot of good ideas are dangerous."

"Not if you go and get yourself killed."

"I'm hard to kill."

"The graveyards are full of men who said they were hard to kill."

"Yeah, well, nobody's gotten me yet. There's only one problem."

"What's that?"

"I don't have a cutting horse or any gear for that sort of work. I ride down into the Thicket without chaps, I'll bleed to death."

"You could talk to old Charles Forester. He was running a good-sized herd before the war, but the Confederacy confiscated every last cow. Last I heard, he hadn't built another herd."

Will nodded. "That's a good idea."

"Thank you, dear husband. And it might be a better idea than you know. Father used to buy workhorses off Mr. Forester because he did a good job breeding and raising them. They weren't thoroughbreds, but they got the job done."

"That's what I need, a horse to get the job done."

"Or you could just stay here."

"Rufus is right, I reckon. Now is the time to get in on the cattle business. Before you know it, the opportunity will pass."

"But you have money."

"Correction: *we* have money."

"It's your money. I didn't have two dimes to rub together when you came back."

"*Two shall become one.* It's our money now."

"All right. Our money, then. Whatever the case, we have it. Why risk your life chasing cattle?"

"Because that money won't last. Even if we only gather a small number of cattle, Rufus and I might still come home with a few double eagles in our pockets."

"Then bandits might set after you."

Will laughed. "What's gotten into you?"

"I told you. I'm worried."

"Well, stop it. Even the Bible says not to worry."

"It also says not to judge others, Mr. Bentley."

"I'm not judging. I'm just reminding you is all. Have faith. Worrying's the opposite of faith."

"How do you figure?"

"Well, faith is believing without seeing, right? Worrying is believing in trouble that might never show up."

"I guess you're right. But you know who's down there in the Thicket."

He nodded.

She said his name anyway. "Teal."

"We'll be careful."

"He killed my family, Will. I can't stand the thought of losing you, too."

"Well, don't think about it, then. The Thicket's a big place, Maggie. We'll keep an ear out. Besides, I know some folks down there from when I used to visit my uncle. They'll tell me if Teal's around."

"What about alligators?"

"What about them?" Will laughed. "I'm hunting cattle, not taking a swim."

"Still, don't you go getting eaten."

"I think a gator would prefer to gobble you up, Mrs. Bentley. Chomp, chomp, chomp."

He leaned close and nipped at her ear.

She giggled, covered instantly in goosebumps. "It appears I have married an insatiable man."

"You're right. Where you're concerned, I am insatiable."

"Good," she said, pulling his head toward her ear again. "Now, take my mind off these worries."

CHAPTER 24

The following afternoon, Sully Weatherspoon was just returning from a ride around the plantation when he saw a black carriage pull up to the estate.

The driver, a stocky thumb of a man, emerged first, his face discolored with faded bruises.

Sheffield, Sully thought, the sight of the man rekindling his rage concerning Will Bentley.

He'd been certain that Gibbs could have handled the job, but that obviously had not been the case. Apparently, Will Bentley had gotten even tougher during the war.

Unconsciously, Sully lifted a hand to his face and ran a fingertip over the crooked contours of his once straight nose.

Well, he wouldn't make the same mistake again. The next time he sent someone after Will Bentley, he'd send enough men to finish the job.

The white-haired Isaac Pew stepped down from his carriage

and climbed the steps toward the front door, leaving the horse and carriage to Sheffield.

Likewise, Sully swung down from his black stallion and called over one of the young black boys loitering outside the stables.

"Take good care of this horse, boy, or you'll wish you were never born."

"Yessir," the frightened boy said, taking the reins.

Sully strode toward the house, not wanting to miss whatever Pew had to say, though he thought he knew exactly why the bitter old man was visiting.

Sully had heard rumors about Rickert hunting for Will Bentley the day before. He couldn't get many details, but he'd heard that Will had faced down Rickert, Pete Smith, and Chad Butler.

That was surprising, since Butler seemed to back down to no man.

There was undoubtedly more to the story.

But that was almost certainly why Pew was here. A man like him hated not getting his way. He was here to beg for the help of Sully's father.

Pew had never endeared himself to the Reconstructionists. He was wealthy enough to make sure they left him alone, but he hadn't spent the time or money to gain real influence among them the way Sully and his father had.

Yes, that's why the old man was here. He wanted the Weatherspoons' influence.

Sully hurried up the steps and through the doors, saw the open door to his father's office, and had just entered when Pew said, "Rickert should be fired."

Sully's father smiled coldly from behind his big desk. "Is that why you're here, Mr. Pew? To ask that I have Rickert removed?"

"No, that's not why I'm here," Pew said, pacing back and forth.

"Ah, son," Mr. Weatherspoon said. "Please join us. You know Mr. Pew, I believe."

"Yes, sir," Sully said, stepping forward, ready to shake the old man's hand. "In fact, I saw Mr. Pew recently, waiting in front of the sheriff's office."

Pew didn't offer to shake hands. Instead, he sneered disdainfully, "Sheriff."

Sully, who had enjoyed plucking the wings from flies as a child, smiled innocently and said, "Yes, sir, Sheriff Rickert."

"Rickert's worthless," Pew said. "Criminally negligent!"

"Son," Mr. Weatherspoon said, and gestured toward one of the chairs in front of his large desk. "Please have a seat. Unless, like our esteemed guest, you would prefer to stand."

"I'll sit, thank you," Sully said, and lowered himself into the chair.

Pew continued to march back and forth. "What I need from you, Weatherspoon, is help doing Rickert's job."

Sully's father smiled politely, feigning ignorance. "Which job, specifically, would that be, Mr. Pew?"

"Running off Will Bentley, of course! Do that, and I'll pay you a hundred dollars."

"Mr. Pew, it's my experience that men like Will Bentley don't run off easily," Sully's father said, holding onto that polite smile.

"Sic the bluebellies on him."

Now, Sully's father frowned. "That might not be possible, I'm afraid."

"Why not? You said they were at your beck and call."

"Beck and call is a stretch, Mr. Pew. But yes, I had a good relationship with Major Forsythe."

"Well, sic Forsythe on Bentley, then. Surely, you could pay him out of the hundred dollars and walk away with a tidy profit. And I'll double the sum if you deliver Bentley's sister to me. She's supposed to be my wife!"

For just a second, Sully could see Father struggle to mask his irritation and contempt. But he managed to hold onto his polite smile and tone. "Like I said, Mr. Pew, I enjoyed a good relationship with Major Forsythe, but unfortunately, Major Forsythe left us. He's been reassigned in the West."

It surprised Sully that Pew didn't know at least this much. Forsythe had been gone for weeks.

Was Pew senile, or had he just grown soft? Was it possible that money had weakened him?

Sully rejected the thought instinctively, knowing that he would never allow anything to dull his own edge.

"Well, bribe whoever's in charge now."

"Culp."

"What?"

"Captain Culp, Mr. Pew. That's the new commander's name."

"I don't care if his name is General Grant. Bribe him. Drive Bentley out of the territory, and bring me his sister, and I'll give you… three hundred dollars!"

"Five hundred," Sully's father said.

"Five hundred?" Pew squawked. "That's ridiculous."

Sully's father spread his hands. "You, of all people, sir, should know the cost of doing business. This new captain isn't as agreeable as Forsythe was. My nephew recently got into trouble. Sully paid Captain Culp a good sum of money. The man left us alone, but he still hung my nephew."

Pew glanced in Sully's direction.

Sully nodded solemnly, thinking how angry his father would be if he knew how things had really worked out behind closed doors. Sully had kept the money and garnished grudging favor from Culp by turning Carter in... a much better arrangement.

"What is the world coming to?" Pew complained, eyes blazing with indignation. "Fine. Get rid of Bentley and bring me his sister, and I'll pay you five hundred dollars."

Sully's father rose from his seat.

Sully did the same.

"I'll consider your request, Mr. Pew," Sully's father said. "But I can provide no guarantees at this time. Where is Bentley staying?"

"Rickert doesn't know," Pew snarled.

"He's a pig farmer, right?" Sully's father asked. "Did Rickert check his farm?"

"A carpetbagger bought the farm, sir," Sully said. He was surprised that his father hadn't known that. There had been a time when Alistair Weatherspoon had known everything that went on in this county, no matter how trivial. When Sully was just a boy, his father had explained that information was the path to power.

But he hadn't known about the Bentley farm selling. Interesting. Perhaps Mr. Pew wasn't the only one growing soft.

"I don't care if he's a pig farmer or a ballerina," Pew snapped. "I want him out of here."

"I'll see what I can do, Mr. Pew," Sully's father said. "But again, no guarantees. If we don't even know where Bentley is, how could we even dispatch Union soldiers?"

"Well, do whatever you have to do," Pew said. "I'm certainly paying you enough to do it."

"Excuse me, Mr. Pew," Sully said.

The old man glared at him. "What is it?"

"Well, sir, it's just that I know Will Bentley. He's a violent man. What if he resists?"

"Not my problem. I want him gone."

"Yes, sir. But what I mean to say, sir, is what if he resists, and he ends up getting killed?"

"All the better. A mad dog like that should be killed. He twisted my ear!"

"I'm terribly sorry to hear that, sir," Sully said, and it was all he could do to keep from laughing.

But he did, indeed, rein in his laughter, and soon after, Mr. Pew said his curt goodbyes and left.

"That," Sully's father said, "is a man consumed by hate. Learn from him, son. The utter foolishness, offering five hundred dollars for the removal of a pig farmer and the possession of a pig farmer's sister. Madness."

Sully nodded. "Madness from which we stand to benefit, sir."

His father shook his head. "I'm not so certain. Bentley could be anywhere."

"We know his general vicinity. He ran off Rickert, didn't he? I could talk to the sheriff and find out where Bentley was."

Sully's father sat down again and tented his fingers before his mouth. "Perhaps. Five hundred dollars is a lot of money. But this Culp…"

"He's a problem, sir."

"How much do you think he would demand?"

"I don't know, sir. He drives a hard bargain. Perhaps two hundred dollars?"

"What's the world coming to?" Sully's father grumbled.

Sully wondered if the man even realized he had echoed the failing Pew.

"We don't need the bluebellies anyway, sir," Sully said.

"Of course we need them."

"For a quarter of what it would cost to bribe Culp, I could hire a gang of good men to ride out there and drive off Bentley," Sully said.

Of course, he would never allow Bentley to escape. He would kill him, have his revenge, and make sure Bentley never shared Sully's biggest secret.

Troublesome things, secrets. Much like this business with Captain Culp. Because although Sully had told his father that he'd bribed the captain, he had indeed kept the money himself.

Meanwhile, he doubted Culp would accept a bribe, no matter how big. The man stunk of duty and honor. Which Sully would never be stupid enough to embrace, but which could nonetheless cause him real trouble if his father insisted that he bribe the captain again.

Offering Culp a bribe might even get Sully thrown in jail. Or worse, hung.

But what would Sully say if his father insisted on his bribing Culp again? He could not risk letting his father know that he

JOHN DEACON

had kept the money, let alone betrayed the location of his cousin.

"I don't want to be lumped in with the troublemakers," his father said. "If you hire men to remove Bentley and word gets back to Culp…"

"It won't, sir. I'll make sure of that."

His father looked at him dubiously. "If I recall, you have your own score to settle with Will Bentley."

"I did, sir."

"Isn't he the one who broke your nose back before the war?"

Sully nodded, hiding his rage. It had always burned him that his father had refused to do anything about that, saying Sully had acted foolishly and earned a valuable lesson that he would be reminded of every time he looked in the mirror. "But that was a long time ago, sir. I have moved past my anger."

His father looked more dubious still. "Is that why you hired Mr. Gibbs to assault Will Bentley?"

Sully was shocked to the core. He never expected Gibbs to betray him. He'd paid Gibbs plenty to avoid that. "If Roy Gibbs said that, he's a liar!"

Sully's father offered an irritating, superior smile. "Mr. Gibbs did not say that. But I am not an idiot, son. Remember that… always."

"I would never think that you were an—"

"We'll see about your old nemesis, Will Bentley," Sully's father interrupted. "Tomorrow, I am heading to New Orleans on business. You will be joining me. Someday, far in the future, I'll be gone, and you'll need to know how to run this plantation. And that means learning business."

"Yes, sir," Sully said, irritated again by his father's implications. Why, Sully was perfectly capable of running this plantation, business and all, without any help from his father.

"But when we return," Mr. Weatherspoon said, "you may go talk to Sheriff Rickert and make whatever inquiries you see fit. If you can locate Will Bentley, perhaps we will take Mr. Pew's money after all. You find out where Bentley is but don't go stirring up any trouble. Folks around these parts like him. He's a war hero."

"War hero," Sully scoffed.

"Yes, war hero. Trust me, son. You don't want folks holding your war record up next to his, do you?"

Sully's face burned with sudden heat. "No, sir."

"All right. Listen to me, and you might learn a thing or two. You have to be smart. You have to think like a politician. That's how you prosper."

"Yes, sir," Sully said, wishing his father would hurry up and quit talking.

"You find out where Bentley is," Sully's father said. "Then leave him be. The bluebellies won't go hunt him down on their own. But if you provide his location, they'll haul him in or run him off. And we'll be hundreds of dollars richer, all without dragging our names into the mix. That's how you take care of things."

"Yes, sir," Sully said again, even managing a smile, but his father clearly didn't understand the situation. Sully had a score to settle with Will Bentley, a personal score that he wouldn't leave to the bluebellies.

CHAPTER 25

Will and Rufus rode slowly through the open gate and toward Charles Forester's home. An old, dust-colored dog coughed a few dispirited barks and retreated under the porch.

Otherwise, the place was empty. There was no movement, no noise. Not a single cow inhabited the pastures or pens. The barn door stood open, revealing only silent darkness within.

"Kind of a spooky place," Rufus whispered.

Will nodded. "Feels like a ghost town."

"Think anybody's here?"

Will shrugged then rode up to the porch and called, "Hello, the house!"

Silence.

Will called again.

Faintly, he heard footsteps inside. The door swung open, and Charles Forester stepped into view.

The cattleman had aged poorly over the several years since

THE PROVIDER

Will had last seen him and had put on a good deal of weight, a rare phenomenon in this place and time. The pistol shoved through his belt jutted at a strange angle, canted by his large belly.

For a moment, Forester just stared at them, white-haired and baggy-eyed, looking tired and suspicious and mildly confused.

Will wondered if maybe the man had gone senile.

But then Forester squinted at him and said, "Will Bentley?"

"Yes sir," Will said. "Good morning, Mr. Forester."

Forester nodded. "Thought that was you. Got big. Who's that with you?"

"My name's Rufus Twill, sir," Rufus said directly... a bold move, given the state of things in Texas.

"All right," Forester said, "you men climb down. I got some coffee left. Hurts my stomach. But I still brew a whole pot fresh every morning. Habit, I guess."

Forester lumbered inside and left the door open behind him.

Will climbed down and hitched his mule. Rufus did the same with his horse.

They went up the steps and hesitated on the porch until Forester called from within, "Come on in, boys."

They followed his voice down a hall to a kitchen, where Forester pulled two mugs from a cabinet and set them on the table and filled them with coffee.

"Sit down, sit down," Forester said, turning to set the pot on the stove again. Stacks of unwashed dishes towered crookedly on the countertop. "You'll excuse my mess. I'm not used to company, and you could say this place lacks a woman's touch."

The men sat down, Will and Rufus with their mugs of

coffee, Forester with an empty tumbler and a jar of amber liquid.

"So what brings you boys here?" Forester said, pouring whiskey into his tumbler.

"Cattle," Will said.

Forester lifted his snowy brows and snorted. "Cattle, huh?" He hoisted the jar. "Want to liven up that coffee, boys?"

"No thank you, sir," Will said.

Rufus also refused politely.

"Suit yourselves. You taste that coffee, you might change your minds. I brew it strong enough to float a skillet on top, and it's been cold for hours."

Will lifted the mug and sipped. The coffee was dark and bitter and cold. But it was still coffee. "Suits me just fine, sir."

"Likewise," Rufus said, sipping his. "Thank you for the coffee, sir."

Forester eyed Rufus for a second. "So you're free now, huh?"

Rufus sat up a little straighter. "Yes, sir."

"Hmm," Forester said noncommittally. "That's different."

"Yes, sir, it is," Rufus said. "I always wanted to be free, and now I am."

"I'll bet. No man wants to live like a milk cow. So... cattle, huh? What about them?"

"We're fixing to go gather some," Will said.

Forester's eyes shifted lazily from Will to Rufus and back to Will. He sipped his whiskey, swallowed, and winced. "Burns my stomach, but I keep drinking it. Habit, I guess. Just the two of you going on this gather?"

"Yes, sir," Will said. "For now, anyway."

"Where do you plan to gather these cattle?"

"The Thicket, sir."

Forester took a belt of whiskey, winced again, and shook his head. "Forget it."

Will just looked at him, waiting for the man to have his say.

"No sense gathering cattle. Somebody will just take them. I used to have a good-sized herd."

"I remember, sir," Will said. "You gave me some work down through the years—roping, branding—when I needed money."

"I remember. You were a good worker. Natural on a horse. Offered you a full-time job, didn't I?"

"Yes, sir."

"But you turned me down. Had the family to care for and the pig farm to run."

"Yes, sir."

Forester nodded and picked up his glass and swirled its contents, staring into the amber liquid with a frown on his tired face. "What happened to the pigs?"

"The Confederacy confiscated them."

Forester nodded. "And the farm?"

"Carpetbagger got it."

"And now you want to gather cattle?"

"Yes, sir."

"The bluebellies will take them."

"We don't aim to keep them long, sir."

"No?"

"No, sir. We aim to drive them to market."

Forester looked up from his glass. For just a split second, Will glimpsed life in the man's eyes, but when Forester spoke, his gaze had gone flat again. "Used to drive them up to Missouri. Then they locked us out on account of tick fever. Where you boys reckon you'll take them, Shreveport?"

"No, sir," Rufus spoke up. "Abilene."

"Abilene?" Forester said. His voice was full of gruff challenge, but Will hadn't noticed another flash of life in his eyes. "Heard Chisholm blazed a trail. Used the Wichita tribe to pack it hard for him. Smart man, Chisholm."

"Yes, sir," Will agreed. "He's a good man."

"You might not think so, you get on that trail of his. You know the trouble with a trail paved by Indians?"

"Indians, sir?"

"That's right. And that's a lot of trouble. One time, after Missouri closed its doors, we took the western trail. Ran into Kiowas and Comanches. It's a wonder any of us even survived. Wouldn't have if there weren't so many of us, and every last man a battling Texan at heart."

Forester polished off his whiskey and poured some more and launched into a lengthy tale of his drive through Indian country and how the Kiowas had stampeded their herd, not once but twice, and stolen some of their horses in the night. And the sheer terror of Comanche raids, the lords of the plains riding down on them, whooping and firing their rifles and bows like horsemen of the apocalypse.

Although Forester was recounting the hardest of hard times, life came into his eyes as he spoke. Not just a flicker this time. His eyes glowed, these memories rekindling something within him.

He rolled up his sleeve, revealing a forearm that was thick with muscle beneath the gray hair. At the once powerful arm's center rose a knot of terrible scar tissue. "That's where the arrow stuck me, but it was a good thing I got the arm up in time, or the thing would have split my heart in two, and then whose cold coffee would you be drinking?"

Forester slapped the table and laughed hoarsely and poured himself some more whiskey. "You boys sure you don't want some? No? All right. Suit yourselves. Remembering the past makes my throat parched. Driving cattle is thirsty work. Hard work. You end up hungry, hot, freezing, tired… all on the same drive. Work like you've never known, driving cattle."

Forester stopped himself then, looking vaguely uncomfortable. "Though you were in the war, weren't you, Will?"

"Yes, sir."

"And you were a slave, Rufus?"

"Yes, sir."

Forester shook his head. "Well, then I suppose you boys have seen your own hard times. You'll have to excuse me. A man reaches a certain age, it seems no one ever had it half so hard as he did in his youth."

"We know driving cattle is hard work, sir," Will said.

"That ain't the half of it, son. Gathering cattle's hard work, too. Especially down in that godawful Thicket. You ever been down there?"

"Yes, sir," Will said. "I had an uncle who lived down there."

Forester raised one brow. "Ever gather cattle down there?"

Will shook his head.

"I have, sir," Rufus said.

Forester turned his attention to Rufus, sizing him up afresh, the way men do when they brush up against another professional. "Tell me about it."

Rufus related his trips into the Thicket, the challenges they'd faced, and rolled back his own sleeve to display scars of his own, permanent welts from thorns and a large, dark scar where a crafty bull had drawn him into a tangled pocket and slashed him with its horn.

Forester laughed. "Those bulls down there are monsters. Some of them, they aren't even cattle, not really. They're prehistoric creatures we don't even have a name for. They're too big to be cattle, too smart, too mean. It's dangerous work, that's for sure."

"I never much minded danger," Will said.

Forester grinned, his eyes glittering with life now. "It's a young man's work, gathering cattle. Especially in the Thicket." He nodded, studying Will again. "But I can see you have fire. Both of you. Tell you what. How about I hire you boys? Money's hard to come by these days, but I got some socked away. I could use two more good men."

"Thank you, Mr. Forester," Rufus said, "but no thank you, sir. We're free men and working for ourselves."

Forester looked at Rufus for a few seconds, filling the room with tension.

Then the old rancher grinned and slapped the table. "Good for you, Rufus. Answered like a true cattleman. By God, if I were a younger man, I'd throw in with you two right now."

Will sipped his cold coffee. "You're welcome to come along, sir."

"Me?" Forester snorted. "Not a chance, son. My gathering days are over. I have arrived at the sitting years. But what brings you here? You didn't come here to sip coffee and hear stories. What can I do for you boys?"

"I'm hoping to buy a horse, sir," Will said. "A good one. And some equipment if you have any to spare."

"Long on grit and short on gear, huh?" Forester laughed. "You got any money?"

"I do, sir."

"Well, then, I'll sell you one of the best horses in Texas. I'll warn you, though. He ain't much to look at. But you won't find a better cutting horse than Clyde. I guarantee that. Horse gets in among mean bulls, he moves like a collie."

"I appreciate that," Will said. "How much would you ask?"

Forester studied them both for a moment. "Tell you what, Will. You've captured my imagination. Your little venture is the most interesting thing I've heard about in quite some time. Whatever capital you've got, you'll need it. Trust me. If there's one thing a cattleman always needs more of than he thinks, it's hard, cold cash. Whether it's for ferrying cattle or passage fees or hiring hands or a trail boss or a good cook, you always need money. You keep your money and pay me in cattle. Bring me twelve head of young stuff, help me brand them, and we'll call it even. I'll even throw in some chaps and whatever else you need. You got gloves?"

"Yes, sir."

"You, Rufus?"

"Yes, sir."

"All right. What about rope then?"

"No, sir," Will said.

"No rope?" Forester laughed. "What were you gonna do, lasso them with a kind word? If you boys aren't something, I don't know what is. You got grit, though. I'll give you that. Not much more than grit, maybe, but I'll tell you something, if you

JOHN DEACON

ain't got grit, you'll never make a cattleman, no matter how much money or gear you got."

Forester launched again into the dangers of the Thicket. The swamps and gators and snakes and the cattle themselves.

"We'll be cautious, sir," Will told him.

"Cautious ain't enough. Look, I got two good men still on the payroll. Fletcher and Hill. Top hands, both of them. Don't know why I even keep them on with no cattle to work. Habit, I guess."

He chuckled humorlessly, shaking his snowy head.

"But I'm sending them with you. Fletcher and Hill, I mean. You want some other men, they can probably point you in the right direction. This country's full of hungry *hombres*, and some of them even know a thing or two about cattle. But that'd be on your dime, you understand, not mine."

"Yes, sir."

Forester nodded, the light in his eyes brighter than ever, having grown almost manic with excitement.

"You sure you don't want to ride with us, sir?" Will asked.

"Me?" Forester laughed. "No, I'm too old and too fat, no matter how much I'd like to ride along. I won't deny that. I would give this whole ranch to go on one more good drive. And by good, I mean all of it. Not just the grub and money. The rain, the snow, the lightning storms, the flash floods, the mean bulls and Indians and bandits… all of it."

Forester shook his head. "But no, I can't ride along. I will send Fletcher and Hill with you, though. They're good men. Top hands. They know cattle, and they know the Thicket. They've never been up Chisholm's new route, but they've both ridden long trails many a time. You couldn't hope for better men."

"Thank you, sir," Will said. "How much for them to ride along?"

"You sure are in a rush to part with your money, Will. I'm not charging you a dime. Not in cash, anyway. Like I said, you'll be needing that. Let's call this a partnership." He glanced at Rufus. "A partnership between free men."

Rufus smiled at Forester's choice of words but still asked the important question. "How would our partnership work, sir?"

"Well, I'm lending you my two best men, and I'll supply some things you need and help you get your herd up the trail. In return, you'll bring me longhorns. I haven't had the grit to go after cattle, not since the bluebellies confiscated the last bunch. First it was the Confederacy, then it was the Union. Knocked the fight right out of me. But you boys have lit a fire in me. Made me realize I want to build up another herd. A small one, anyway. I miss hearing them and smelling them, getting out there and cussing at them. I miss going to town and chewing the fat with men over at the feed store. All I do now is sit here and drink whiskey and pay men to live in my bunkhouse. Well, I'm fixing to change that. I'm gonna have some cattle. Life isn't hardly worth living without being able to look out the window and see some longhorns. And if the bluebellies steal my cattle again, I'll get some more. Or who knows? Maybe this time, now that I got my fire back, I'll stand up to them Yankees and tell them to gather their own cattle."

"You do that, sir, you let me know, and I'll stand with you," Will said.

"I'll just bet you would, son. I'll just bet you would. But

listen, speaking of trouble, you go down there in the Thicket, you're gonna have to watch out for something I never had to mess with."

"Raiders?"

Forester nodded. "Raiders, marauders, murderers, whatever you want to call them. I hear there's a bunch of them boys hiding out down there. You better keep your eyes open, or you'll just be gathering cattle for some gang of no-good, murdering thieves giving the gray a bad name. You better be ready to fight."

"I'm always ready to fight, sir," Will said.

"I'll bet you are," Forester said. "Fletcher and Hill can both fight, too. You won't have to worry about them. Good men. Top hands. I'm glad I kept them around after all. But you just watch yourselves. Some of those gangs are downright savage, from what I hear."

Will nodded in agreement. "You ever hear of a man named Teal?"

Forester nodded grimly. "Guerrilla fighter gone bad. Got ice water in his guts and fire in his skull. A real hard case. He'd shoot his own mother for a chew of plug."

Will nodded. "He's a mad dog."

"And he's down there where you're fixing to go, last I heard. You got something personal against the man?"

Will nodded, picturing the charred ruins of Maggie's house. "Yes, I do. He killed my wife's family. Burned them out and shot them when they tried to escape the flames."

"You marry the Dunne girl?"

"Yes, sir, I did."

"Good for you. I used to sell her daddy a horse from time to time. She's a pretty thing. Reddest hair I ever seen. Good on a horse, too. She can really ride."

"Yes, sir, she can."

"Shame, what happened to her people. Real shame."

"Yes, sir."

Forester studied him again, looking almost wary. "You're not going into that Thicket for revenge, are you? Because if that's what you're up to, I won't send my men."

"I'm going after cattle, sir, not Teal."

But of course, he thought, *if I happen to run into Teal while I'm down there, that's another story.*

"Good," Forester said. "That's good. The deal stands then. You go down there, gather your cattle, bring them back, tell me all about it. I get your first dozen cattle, Will, to pay for that ugly horse I'm about to sell you."

"Yes, sir, if he's as good a cutting horse as you say."

"That good and better. You've never seen a cattle horse like Clyde. But ugly?" Forester shook his head. "You won't be getting any compliments on his lines, that's for sure."

"That's all right, sir. I just need a good cattle horse."

"And you'll have him. I'll lend you some other horses, too. You boys'll need more than one a day down there. But Clyde'll be yours. Then I get your first dozen head of cattle. How are you boys splitting your gather, if you don't mind me asking?"

"Right down the middle," Will said. "Fifty-fifty."

Forester nodded. "Rufus, I suppose that means you get the second dozen. That work for you?"

"Yessir," Rufus said.

"Then, we'll split what's left down the middle. Half'll go to you boys, half'll come to me. And trust me. That's a bargain.

Fletcher and Hill won't just do their share. They'll triple the size of your gather and teach a lot along the way. Gumption's good, but nothing beats experience."

Will and Rufus agreed to the terms and thanked Forester, and the men stood and shook hands, and they went outside to get Fletcher and Hill, the gear, and the cutting horse.

Will just hoped this Clyde was half as good as Forester said.

CHAPTER 26

"Meet Clyde," Forester said, nodding to the stallion cropping grass in a pasture behind the barn.

"Clyde, huh?" Will said, studying the gigantic, over muscled horse with its huge, ungainly head. "What's his last name, Dale?"

"He's a biggun, but he works cattle like no other horse you ever saw."

Will walked over to the rail close to where the big horse was munching on grass. Clyde was a blue roan with a coat the washed-out blue-gray color of an old gun barrel. Darker spots spattered this unremarkable color in shotgun-blast patterns. Overall, he was lighter in the hind quarters and almost black in the face and chest and the upper part of his neck, which gave him the appearance of a horse standing half in shadow. His mane was black and wild.

"Well, Clyde," Will said, "you're ugly enough to be a good

worker, anyway. You want to go down into the Thicket with me and gather some cattle?"

The horse lifted his head a little and stared at Will with a bright eye that Will had to admit was full of intelligence.

Will stood and stuck out his hand to Forester. "All right, you got a deal. You told the truth about him being ugly. I'll trust that you're telling the truth about the rest, too."

"Oh, I'm telling the truth all right. And if I wasn't so old and heavy, I wouldn't sell him to you for ten times what I'm asking. Only reason I'm selling him at all is it breaks my heart to see a good horse go to seed in a corral. Horse like Clyde needs to work. You take him down there, you'll see. That horse'll practically rope and brand cattle on his own."

"All right," Will laughed. "I bought, so you can quit selling, Mr. Forester. I'll see what old Clyde's made of soon enough."

From there, they ambled over to the tack room, and Forester gathered gear for Will.

"You'll need a working saddle," Forester said. "Here, take this one. And here."

Next, Forester took down a pair of thick, fringed shotgun chaps dyed black. "Take these. They're my own chaps. I hate to give them to you because it's like admitting I'll never ride again."

Will waved him off. "You go ahead and keep them, then."

Forester shook his head. "You take them. You're too tall for any of the other pairs. I doubt they'd have anything to fit you in town, and now you got me all fired up about this gather. I don't want to have to sit around waiting for you to get some chaps made. Take them."

Will nodded and took the chaps and thanked him.

"Don't mention it," Forester said. "You are leaving soon, aren't you? For the gather, I mean?"

"Yes, sir. As soon as possible. When could your men go?"

"How about tomorrow morning at daybreak? You get here before that, I'll feed you. But don't expect much talk from Fletcher or Hill. They're all business."

"That works," Will said.

"You boys armed?"

"To the teeth."

"Good. I'll make sure Fletcher and Hill are, too. You want them to get some other hands to join you?"

Will looked at Rufus.

Rufus shrugged. "That's your call, Will. I don't got any money. You hire them, I'll pay you back once we get to market."

Will nodded and turned back to Forester. "What's your recommendation, sir?"

"Hire them. I wouldn't go down there without at least six good men, maybe more. It'll cost you, though. Probably two dollars a day for the sort of men you want."

"I can do that," Will said.

"All right. I'll tell Fletcher and Hill to round up some men. How many do you want to hire?"

Will did some quick math in his head. "How long do you reckon a gather like that will take?"

"Heh. You never know, son. Might be you head down there and round up a nice little herd in two days' time. Might be you spend two weeks down there and don't come back with enough cattle to pay off old Clyde here."

"I'll hire four men if they can be ready tomorrow," Will said.

"That shouldn't be a problem. Lots of good men with no way to feed their families now," Forester said. "Can I tell them you're offering two dollars a day, or do you want to haggle with them?"

"No haggling," Will said. Eight dollars a day would add up quickly, but he had the money, and if these men each gathered even a few head of cattle each day, he'd still make a staggering profit. "I'll pay."

Forester smiled, clearly pleased by Will's answer. "Good. A cattleman needs to think big and swagger. He does nothing by half measure."

Will grinned. "I'm not a cattleman."

"That's what you say now, Will. You just wait until the end of the drive. You're a cattleman. I can see it in your eyes."

"All right," Will said, figuring there was no sense in arguing the point. All he wanted to do was take care of his family. If Forester wanted to imagine Will was some natural-born cattleman, so be it.

"And you'll feed them?" Forester asked.

Will could have slapped himself. He was so used to fending for himself and packing a light horse, he hadn't even thought of food. "Yeah, I'll feed them. Though I don't know how, exactly. I suppose we might have to delay this gather after all."

"No, no," Forester said. "You go ahead and borrow my chuck wagon. I got enough supplies to see you through. If you're hiring extra men and I'm getting half the gather, it's only right I feed the lot of you. But you men'll have to fend for yourselves. My cook got killed in the war."

"All right," Will said. "I appreciate it."

"I got a good feeling about this," Forester said, clapping him on the back. "And not just this venture. About you. And you, too, Rufus. Both of you. I got a feeling I'm witnessing the birth of a pair of real Texas cattlemen."

CHAPTER 27

By the time they reached the Thicket, Will and the men had already rounded up forty-two unbranded head, mostly young stuff.

They pushed them into the Thicket, where the real work began.

After a week of hard work, beating the brush and working the brakes along the Sulfur from dawn to dusk, they had chased out two hundred and fifty-two head of wild cattle, bringing their herd to within spitting distance of three hundred, a number far greater than Will had expected.

It had been quite a week for him. Grueling, yes, but far more exciting than he could have ever imagined.

He'd always been at home atop a horse, and these were good horses—especially Clyde, who had proven Forester an honest man.

The blue roan had no quit in him and moved like an extension of Will's consciousness, doing the work at hand even as it came into Will's mind.

Clyde knew when to press a cow, when to flank them, and when to dodge a mean bull's horns. And there was no shortage of mean bulls in the Thicket.

These old mossyhorns were the far-flung descendants of cattle abandoned hundreds of years earlier by the Spanish, and they had adapted over the years into creatures utterly at home in the canebrakes and pine groves and occasional grassy meadows as gators were to the hyacinth-clogged bayous that came in and out of the riders' view.

From time to time, a startled cow would stumble into one of these bogs. Will would rope her, the action second nature to him as a longtime rider and veteran cavalryman. Then Clyde, or whatever horse Will was riding at the time—for even though the stallion showed no signs of exhaustion, Will was careful to rest him from time to time—would dig in and drag the blatting cow back to dry ground.

All of the horses knew the work, but Clyde ruled supreme. In these moments, he would hunker like a mustang sliding down a slope of loose shale, and his big muscles would tense, going hard as stone as he forced his will on the floundering animal.

Forester also hadn't exaggerated the skill of Fletcher and Hill, nor had he assumed too much of the men they'd brought along, four Mexican vaqueros born to the saddle.

The days were long and exhausting, and the men and horses were all torn by thorns and cut by cane. Rufus had been unseated by a low-hanging limb but pushed through the pain, and one afternoon, Will had been charged by the biggest boar he'd ever seen.

The thing came charging out of the cane, its long tushes flashing like a pair of fixed bayonets, rushing straight at Clyde's shanks.

Before Will could even pull his Colt and bring his sights onto the big boar, the stallion reared and brought down his hoof with tremendous force, smashing the pig's skull with the iron horseshoe and killing the boar instantly.

The incident impressed Will and the others and gave them some fresh meat that was a nice break from the salt pork and beans they'd been eating for every meal since leaving home.

Nights when he wasn't watching the herd, Will would sit by the fire, thoroughly exhausted, swapping stories with the other men or just sit there, staring into the flames, listening to the night guard sing their soothing songs to the drowsing cattle. During these quiet times, Will's mind drifted home. He missed Maggie and his family and hoped they were okay but stopped short of worrying. Fretting did no good, of course, plus he suspected they were fine.

After all, none of those who might come hunting him in his absence—Rickert, Pew's men, the Weatherspoons, or the bluebellies—had any cause to bother the women. They had done nothing.

And if someone did trouble them, well, the women had Mama's shotgun and the derringers.

He had considered leaving the Dragoon behind, too, but had let Rufus borrow it instead.

After all, Teal and men like him were down here in the

Thicket, not to mention the garden-variety bandits he knew lurked here and there among the pines.

They hadn't encountered many folks during their time here, and most of those had been friendly enough, but a few times, men had stared like hungry wolves from a distance and skulked away into the brush when Will had hailed them.

These men were uniformly dirty, ragged, and bearded. Will reckoned they feared the drovers' number and firepower, but the return trip might prove downright interesting.

Give those swamp rats time to band up, they might try an ambush.

But again, it wasn't a thing to worry over. Will just stayed ready and made sure they had a guard posted all night.

The real danger, of course, was Teal.

When they'd first ridden into the Thicket, Will found himself hoping they'd cross paths with the murderer. He ached to avenge the deaths of Maggie's family and others like them. Then there was the bank, of course, and all the hard-earned money Teal had stolen from Will and others. Beyond that, it enraged him, a man like Teal robbing and raping and spilling innocent blood while still wearing the gray.

Through four years of battle, Will and the other men of the Fifth had battled valiantly and honorably, fighting in support of a higher ideal, the defense of their republic and freedom against an invading army.

Teal's crimes were a mockery of those sacrifices, those ideals. They were nothing short of treasonous. Not against the Confederacy, exactly, since the Confederacy was dead and dust, but the Republic of Texas and those ideals for which Will and his brothers-in-arms had fought over those long four years.

So yes, he wanted very badly to kill Teal.

But the longer they were in the Thicket, the more this urge abandoned him, and by this night, a week into things, with a herd of nearly three hundred head bedded down nearby, lowing softly, Will had begun to hope that they wouldn't clash with Teal this trip but another time instead.

That, of course, is the trouble with having something to lose. It makes you cautious. And having gathered six thousand dollars' worth of cattle, Will had plenty to lose.

"What do you think about turning back tomorrow?" he asked Rufus after the others had stretched out on their bedrolls.

"You missing Maggie, partner?" Rufus asked with a grin.

"You know I am, my friend. But that's not my main reason."

"You don't want to push our luck?"

"Something like that."

"Every day, we're chasing out thirty or forty head of cattle. That's a lot of money, partner."

Will nodded. "It is. But every day is also a chance to run into raiders and lose everything."

Rufus nodded. "How much money we made, do you reckon?"

"By my count, fifty-seven of those cattle are mine. A hundred and twenty-six belong to Forester. And sixty-nine are yours."

Rufus's smile gleamed in the firelight. "How much money is that?"

"Your share?"

"Right. I know I owe you some money for the men."

"Drop in the bucket compared to what the cattle are worth."

"Which is?"

"We get them all to market, your share will come to around fourteen hundred dollars. Maybe even more."

Rufus's eyes grew huge. "Is that much even possible?"

"Yes, sir, it is. That being said, I figure we should give each of these men a cut. They hired on for their wages, but we couldn't have done this without them, and I'd like their help again."

"You want to come back here, do this again?"

"I do."

"So old Forester was right. You're a cattleman in the making."

"So are you."

"That's all I ever wanted to be since the first time I roped a steer," Rufus confessed. "Fourteen hundred dollars. That's a lot of money, Will."

"It is. What are you going to do with it?"

"I don't know. My mind doesn't really work that way. Guess I never expected to have anything of my own really, except maybe a family."

"Is that something you want?"

"Oh yeah. I got a young lady I'd like to marry."

"Does she know that?" Will asked, letting the hint of a smile tug at the corners of his mouth.

"Oh, she knows, all right. Her name's Candy. She loves me."

"Is she soft in the head?"

"Soft in the head? No… why would you…?" Then Rufus's smile came back. "Oh, I get it. You're having a little fun with me. No, for your information, Candy is not soft in the head. Though she probably thinks that I think she is."

"Why's that?"

"I tried to talk her into quitting her job and leaving with me.

Told her what good was freedom if she didn't use it? Free or not, she's still back at that house, slaving away, just like she always has."

Suddenly, Will realized what Rufus was implying. "Does she work for…"

Rufus nodded, his face somber. "The Weatherspoons."

"I'm sorry to hear that, my friend."

"So am I. But we drive these cattle home, I'm gonna ask her to marry me. Then, we get them to market, maybe I'll buy me a ranch like yours and hire folks to do all my work for me, walk around in fancy clothes."

Will grinned. "A real gentleman rancher. Have a hot toddy for breakfast every morning."

"Yeah," Rufus laughed. "That'd be the life. Tell you the truth, Will, so long as Candy'll marry me and we got food on the table, I don't care where we live. I'll be happy."

"Well, with your share of the take, you should have no problem doing that," Will said. "In fact—"

"Hold it right there," a man in the darkness shouted. "We got you surrounded."

CHAPTER 28

Instinctively, Will rolled backward off the stone he'd been sitting on, away from the dying embers, and scooped up his short-barreled scattergun.

An instant later, Rufus was on the ground beside him.

The men stirred in their bedrolls. Out by the cattle, more voices were shouting.

And now another man spoke from behind Will. "He ain't kidding, you boys. We got you covered from all angles. My men, sound off!"

One by one, men called out from the darkness, moving clockwise around the camp's perimeter, fourteen of them in all, covering Will and his friends from all angles.

Was this Teal?

Will tensed, knowing he didn't have a chance. His only hope would be to turn on the men behind him, unload both barrels before they knew what happened, and charge in that direction, hoping to break through the line and escape into the bayou.

But what of the others?

Rufus might follow, but the others would get cut down. Of course, so would Will and Rufus, likely.

They were beaten.

As if reading his mind, the voice in the darkness called out, "Now, you know I'm telling the truth. Look, we don't want to have to kill you boys. Put down your weapons and move toward the fire. We already got your night guard tied up."

As Will listened, his bitterness shifted to curiosity. That voice...

"Come on now, you bunch of Jonahs. You're whipped. Put down your guns, lift your hands high, and step into the light, or we're gonna fill you full of lead."

Bunch of Jonahs, Will thought. *Fill you full of lead...*

Will laid down his scattergun then lifted his hands into the air and stood. "Do as he says, men. The last thing I want my tombstone to read is *'Killed by Benny Braxton.'* Talk about an inglorious epitaph."

"What?" the voice in the darkness called back, sounding surprised. "Who are you? How do you know my name?"

"You spend three years riding with a man, you get to know his voice," Will called back. "I'm a little perturbed that you don't recognize mine."

"Will?" Benny Braxton said, stepping into the flickering light of the dying fire. "Will Bentley?"

"That's right, Benny. It's me. Are you still going to shoot me?"

"Will!" Benny said, stepping forward to embrace Will. "What in the world are you doing down here in the Thicket?"

"I was fixing to ask you the same thing."

"We got some catching up to do, brother," Benny said. Then he called into the darkness, "Come out, men. And tell Juan to let that picket go."

A moment later, Benny's men stepped into the light. They were ragged and wraithlike, starved down beneath their gray uniforms.

They and Will's crew eyed each other warily, but no one made any threats.

"Men," Benny said, "this fella is my brother. Will Bentley, these are the men I ride with now. Sons of the Confederacy, every last one of them."

Three of the men stepped forward immediately to shake Will's hand. They knew him, and he knew them. At least in passing.

Another, younger man stepped forward, something like awe shining in his eyes. "You're Will Bentley? Really?"

"That's right."

"The same Will Bentley that led the charge at the river depot?"

Will nodded.

"The same Will Bentley who got behind the bluebellies up in Indian Country?"

"That's him, boys," Benny announced, a big smile splitting his black beard now as he clapped Will on the shoulder. "This here is the genuine article, Will Bentley."

And just like that, all tension left the moment. Benny's raiders gathered around, jockeying for the opportunity to shake Will's hand and introduce themselves.

He had put the war behind him, but clearly, he was not forgotten by all.

"What are you doing out here, Benny?" Will asked again.

"Like I said, brother, we have a lot to catch up on. But I'll give you the short of it. We all had trouble with the bluebellies at one time or another."

"I heard what happened up at Bonham. I'm glad you're alive."

Benny nodded. "Obliged. If it weren't for the good Lord, I never would've made it out of that scrape. Truth be told, I still don't know how I did."

"You always were a lucky so-and-so," Will laughed.

"Yeah, I don't feel so lucky these days. Mostly what I feel is hungry. These men are in the same boat. They all had trouble like mine, here and there. We all sort of fell in together over time."

"And now what?" Will asked. "Are you highwaymen?"

"I'm sorry about this whole thing, Will. We saw you boys with all them cattle and figured we could use some beef. If I had known it was you—"

"Don't worry about it, Benny. These are desperate times. And nobody got hurt. Tell you what. Let's throw some wood on that fire and get some grub going. We can catch up over beans and salt pork."

CHAPTER 29

"Where is Will Bentley?" Sully Weatherspoon demanded from atop his black stallion. His men stayed back a few feet, Gibbs on one side and Chad Butler, whom Sully had hired after speaking with that nincompoop Sheriff Rickert, on the other.

The old man stood there, barefoot, fooling with the straps of his filthy bib overalls, and took his time answering, which infuriated Sully. But such things one must endure when dealing with peasants, and Sully's father had forbidden him to cause trouble out here.

After squinting at Sully for several seconds, the old man spat a long stream of tobacco juice onto the ground between them. "Ain't seen old Will since before the war."

"But you know he's back," Sully said. "Tell me where to find him, old man."

After an even longer pause, the man spat again. "Young man like you ought to call me sir, not old man."

"I said what I said. Where's Bentley?"

"Gone."

"Gone? Gone where?"

"The Thicket."

"You lie. He came back here."

"Came back, sure. Then he left again. Went to the Thicket is what I hear. See, folks around here, we like Will. He comes and goes, we know. He's a good man. Common as dirt, always with a kind word for—"

"I don't care about any of that," Sully snapped. "Why did he go to the Thicket?"

"Will's got friends down there. Good friends. Men who rode together during the... well, maybe you heard of it... the war?"

Sully nearly struck the man then. Of course, there was no way that this man, who didn't know his identity, let alone his personal history, could know about the war. But he'd implied something resembling the truth nonetheless... and it infuriated Sully more even than the man's slack-jawed insolence.

"Watch your mouth, old man. You don't want to make me angry."

The old man gave an aggravating smile, showing Sully a handful of tobacco-stained teeth. "Well, ain't you the cock of the walk? You stick around, maybe Will'll come back and teach you some manners. Of course, he already did teach you some manners, didn't he? All three of you."

The man spat again, fire coming into his eyes.

And that was not only irritating but confounding. How dare this old man display anger while facing three strong young men?

It was breeding. Or rather, lack of breeding. These peasants were stupid and rebellious by nature. It was in their blood.

And Texans were the worst of them.

Sully had enjoyed his time with Father in New Orleans. The town was still reeling from the war, of course, but the wealthy always found a way, and well-to-do Louisianans smart enough not to involve themselves in the war had done a good job of maintaining a secret society that still insulated them from the outer suffering and afforded them all the things befitting their station: good food, good drink, beautiful women to use, and best of all, servants who knew their station, showing great men like Sully all due respect... the exact opposite of detestable men like this Texan peasant.

But now this old man had said something truly surprising. How did he know about...

"That's right," the old man said defiantly. "I know who you are. You're Alistair Weatherspoon's boy."

Sully was shocked. How could this peasant possibly know his name?

"And you," the old man said, pointing a bony finger at Gibbs, "Will taught you a lesson over by the mercantile a week or two back. Heard all about it. You came at him with brass knuckles. Didn't do you much good, did they?"

"It was a lucky punch," Gibbs growled.

"Yeah," the old man laughed. "Sounds like it was a whole bunch of lucky punches. My wife's cousin was there. Said it took them a good fifteen minutes to wake you up. And you."

The old man turned to Chad Butler, who stared daggers back at him. "You're Slim Butler's kid, but I can't say you got much of your daddy in you. From what I hear, you're a cold-blooded killer and fast with that shooting iron of yours. But you ain't no match for Will. He's got the difference."

"The only difference he had was a scattergun," Butler said. "If he would have faced me like a man, he'd be dead."

"Like a man, huh?" the old timer chuckled. "Let me tell you something. Will Bentley is twice the man as all three of you rolled together."

"I don't like your attitude, old man," Butler said, dropping a hand to the butt of his Colt.

"No, Chad," Sully said quickly. "As much as I would enjoy teaching this insolent old peasant a lesson, he's not worth the time or trouble."

"Old peasant, huh? You town boys come out here, stomp around, act important, think we're stupid. Well, maybe we ain't half so stupid as you think. Why do you think I wasted my time standing out here, talking with the likes of you? I was giving my boy time to get into position. You just look back behind me now. Look back there. Should be in the hay loft. Wait for it."

Sully's eyes went to the open door of the hay loft and saw nothing. This old man wasn't just stupid. He was crazy, too.

But then the clouds shifted, and Sully saw sunlight winking off something metallic back there in the loft.

Butler removed his hand from his pistol. "He's telling the truth, boss. Somebody up in that loft has a rifle on us."

"I believe that concludes our business together, boys," the old man said and spat again. "You do yourselves a favor, head on back to town, and stay there. You come out here looking for trouble, you might just find it. In spades."

With that, the man showed them his back and stalked off.

"I'd like to punch that old man in the face," Gibbs said.

"He had the drop on us today," Butler said. "Next time, he won't see me coming."

"Forget that stupid old man," Sully said. "We're here to find Will Bentley."

They rode from farm to farm, but no one would help them. Most of the peasants feigned ignorance, pretending to be clueless hayseeds.

Even though these people addressed Sully respectfully, he detected surly attitudes barely concealed under their polite words and empty smiles.

They knew where Bentley was. They just wouldn't tell Sully.

And for some infuriating reason, they seemed to find the whole thing amusing. Seemed, even, to think that Will might somehow have the upper hand, which was ridiculous.

Things continued this way throughout the morning. The sun crept toward its apex. The day grew hot.

Sully was just about to quit when they came to the one place they knew Will Bentley wouldn't be... his old family farm, which had, amusingly, been snatched up for back taxes by a Yankee carpetbagger.

"Yeah, I know where he is," the carpetbagger said. "You men going to run him off? I don't like him. And I don't like the way he looks at me!"

"Where is he?" Sully demanded, full of triumph.

"Right next door. Though I ain't seen him for a while."

Sully was confused. "Next door? You mean the Dunne place? I heard they burned that."

Inwardly, he chuckled to himself. *Heard they burned it...*

The man couldn't possibly know that Sully had hired the

Teal gang to burn out the Dunnes after their daughter had refused Sully's advances and publicly shamed him.

Jafford Teal was a useful man. A mercenary with no soul.

When the economy collapsed, Father had hired Teal to "rob" the bank. As directed, Teal and his men struck the bank at the appointed time, killed the tellers, and set the place afire.

Teal, of course, was confused not to find the bank manager, Godfrey Simmons, and angry when he discovered only worthless confederate money inside.

Father had already started to spread the rumor that ultimately redirected the rage of the bloodthirsty mercenary: that Godfrey Simmons had, knowing the bank was about to shutter its doors, run off with all the gold, greenbacks, and precious items locked within the vault.

Little did Teal or anyone else know, Father had already killed Simmons, who had foolishly considered father a friend and taken him into the vault early that morning to retrieve his personal wealth.

Father had coordinated everything perfectly. He killed the bank manager, stole everything worth anything, then slipped away well before first light the very morning he knew Teal and his men would ride into town upon the bank's opening, kill everyone inside, and burn the evidence.

Sully was proud of his father for that.

That's how the Weatherspoons had secured themselves against hard times: through forward thinking, expert planning, and flawless execution.

Later, after the lovely but insolent Maggie Dunne had disgraced him, Sully, inspired by his father, had hired Teal to do his bidding, too, and Teal and his raiders had burned out the

Dunnes and shot them as they tried to escape the flames, just as Sully had told him to.

The public, of course, had believed the rumor that Sully had carefully spread. Teal's gang had burned out the Dunnes because Maggie's father had worn the blue.

In reality, Teal didn't care about anything except blood and money, which made him incredibly valuable to Sully.

"No, not the one that burned," the carpetbagger said. "He's shacked up over there, on the other side of the creek, with I think his mother and sister and that red-haired woman."

Sully was thunderstruck.

"Red-haired woman? What red-haired woman?"

"I don't know her name. She's a very attractive young woman. Reddest hair you've ever seen."

The carpetbagger could be describing only one person: Maggie Dunne, the woman who'd broken Sully's heart and humiliated him, the same woman he'd hired Teal to kill.

Sully filled instantly with conflicting emotions. Cold fury met red-hot desire, unleashing a cataclysmic storm within him.

Ignoring the carpetbagger, he turned and rode in the direction the Yankee had pointed.

If Maggie Dunne still lived, he would have her… no matter what.

CHAPTER 30

⚜

"You don't have to escort us," Will told Benny the next morning after breakfast. "I appreciate the offer, but I hate to put you at risk."

"Pshaw!" Benny said. "I'd welcome a little risk right now. We've been sitting around the Thicket too long. And I'm serious, Will. You try riding out here without us, you'll have trouble. Those men you saw, they've ambushed folks before."

"Well, then, I appreciate you and your boys riding along, Benny."

After a meal of pork and beans, the raiders had made camp among Will and his friends, and this morning, after breakfast—pork and beans again—the men had continued the previous night's conversations.

Mostly, it was the raiders wanting to know what was happening back in the world and especially the regions from which they hailed.

In a few cases, notes and addresses were met by promises to deliver messages discreetly to loved ones.

"How many head of cattle do you want?" Will asked.

The raiders looked at Benny, their eyes sharp in their drawn faces.

"You keep your cattle, Will. You boys gathered them."

"Nope. I'm giving you cattle. Friend to friend."

"Well, I sure do appreciate that, Will. All the boys do, I'm sure." Those close by nodded.

"When you're a renegade," Benny said, "it's difficult getting enough to eat. And we don't have the right gear or know how for a gather, either. A couple head of cattle would help us a lot."

"I'll give you four, then. You boys look pretty starved down. And next time we come this way, I'll bring you some flour and such."

Benny shook Will's hand, and his men gathered around to thank him.

"Let's cut out four nice head for these boys," Will told his own people. "And in case any of you are feeling prickly, don't. These cattle come out of my take."

"No sir," Rufus said, stepping forward. "You can give them two, and I'll give them two."

"No," Fletcher said. He was the best, most experienced cowboy in the bunch. "Mr. Forester'll pay his share, too. He's been over the trail enough times to know the cost of doing business. Will, Rufus, you each contribute a cow, and we'll take two out of Forester's double share."

"Works for me," Will said. "All right. Let's round up some nice cattle for these boys."

Will's men started for their horses.

Before Will could join them, Benny stopped him.

"Hey, Will, before you go, I want to show you something."

He drew him away from the others in a private opening behind a rank of ragged pines.

"What is it, Benny?"

"You ever hear of Cullen Baker?"

"Yeah, been hearing his name a lot lately. Heard he's been causing a lot of trouble."

"Don't believe it," Benny said. "Well, don't believe all of it. Old Cullen's got a temper on him, that's for sure. But he didn't do half the stuff folks try to pin on him. I've ridden with him a few times down here, and he strikes me as a good enough man."

"All right. What about him?"

"He taught me something."

"What's that?"

"Something you ought to know how to do yourself. Step back a second, and I'll show you."

Will took a step back and waited. He didn't have to wait long.

Benny dropped a hand to his hip, brushing his coat aside in the process, and brought it back up in a flash... filled with shooting iron.

"That was awful quick," Will said. "How'd you do that?"

"Cullen showed me. And I've practiced a lot."

Keenly interested, Will stared at his friend. "I'm listening."

"Old Cullen's been in a few scrapes. More than a few, if you want to know the truth. And he always comes out on top. According to Cullen, that's because he's perfected his fast draw."

"You mean pulling out a revolver and getting it on target quickly?"

"That's exactly what I mean. You remember when we started the war, nobody carried a revolver."

Will nodded.

"Well, now you see them all the time," Benny said. "Used to be, back in the war, men carried them in their saddle holsters. But now, they're shoving them through their belts like you."

"But not you."

"No sir, not me," Benny said. "Got a holster for my belt. I can get my gun into action faster that way. Especially after practicing."

"Practicing what, exactly?"

"That's what Cullen showed me," Benny said, "and it's what I'm fixing to show you."

An hour later, when they came walking around the pines to rejoin the others, Will was soaked with sweat, and his hand was tired from drawing the Colt over and over and over.

"Thank you, Benny. That was amazing. I'm already twice as fast as I was."

"You keep practicing, you'll be twice as fast again. And if you get yourself a holster, you'll be even faster."

"I'll do that," Will said. His mind was buzzing. It had never occurred to him, just as it had never occurred to most men of his time, that developing a quick draw would make him so much deadlier.

But that was obvious now… and made him wonder just how fast he could get. He was already as quick as Benny. If he practiced a little every day, there was no telling how fast he would be.

"Cullen says times are changing," Benny said. "He says someday soon, every man west of the Mississippi will have a gun on him at all times. A handgun, not a rifle. Cullen says things'll get bad quick for a while. Gunmen will rise. All because they're fast. Then, over time, other folks will catch on or start carrying shotguns. But the point is, you don't want to get caught unawares after folks start practicing and building up their speed. You want to speed up your draw now, so you can live long enough to see how things go. Especially with all the trouble you're having back home."

Will had explained his troubles with Pew and Sully and mentioned that the bluebellies might even come after him. There was one thing he hadn't mentioned yet, not wanting to speak the man's name in front of the riders, some of whom might have mixed loyalties.

Will stopped his friend shy of camp, where the others were talking and packing up and getting ready to ride.

"You know Jafford Teal?" Will asked.

Benny frowned. "Man's a scoundrel. Meaner than a cottonmouth. What about him?"

"He burned out my wife's family."

"I'm sorry to hear that, Will."

"Killed everybody but my Maggie. She wasn't home when they burned the house, otherwise she'd be dead, too. Stole their horses, too. Maggie's father had a nice stable of fine thoroughbreds."

"That's where Teal got that beautiful horse of his, then," Benny said. "I'd wondered. I'm awful sorry that happened, my friend. Teal is a demon in cav boots."

"Yes, he is. I hear he's in the Thicket."

Benny nodded.

"You ever see him?" Will asked.

"Once. We brushed up against him and his boys. Tense moment. Could've gone either way. But nobody unloaded. Guess it was an enemy of enemy thing. We both hate the bluebellies, after all. But if I'd known that he'd burned out your wife's family..."

"No way you could have known, my friend. Any idea where he is down here?"

Benny shook his head. "You can't go after him anyway, Will. He's got eighteen or twenty men riding with him, and they're all hard as nails. Every now and then they'll lynch a scalawag or take a crack at a bluebelly, just to say they're fighting the good fight, but mostly, they're just robbing common folks. Point is, they're a bad bunch. And you go looking for Teal, you'll have to face all of them. That would be a death sentence—even for you, Will, even if you got your quick draw down. There's too many of them, and they're ready to kill, every last one of them."

"I appreciate the warning," Will said. "You say you ran into him, right? Did you talk with him?"

"A little. He asked me about the war, who I rode with. Mostly, he wanted to know if I heard of any bluebellies on the move."

"What's he look like?"

"He's older than you'd think. Maybe forty or forty-five? Little, wiry fella. Mean face with a hawklike nose and hawklike eyes. That's what he made me think of, perched up on the fine horse of his: a cold-eyed hawk, ready to make a kill."

"What color hair?"

"Kind of a reddish-brown, I'd say, and a sandy-colored

beard with a good deal of gray in it. You know who he looks like, now that I think of it?" Benny laughed. "It's pretty ironic."

"Who?"

"General Sherman, the man who burned the South."

A clear image filled Will's mind. Everyone south of the Mason-Dixon Line knew what the dreaded and much hated General William Tecumseh Sherman looked like.

"Thanks, Benny. That's a help."

"You ain't gonna go hunting him are you, Will? If you are, we'll ride with you. At least I will. Most of the boys'll come along. We won't all ride back out, but we'll stand with you."

"I appreciate it, Benny. I really do. But no, I got cattle to drive. Someday, though, I will kill Jafford Teal for what he did to my wife's people. That's a promise. Anybody messes with my family, they die.

CHAPTER 31

Maggie was doing laundry in the creek, humming happily to herself, when she looked up and saw the horsemen riding her way.

For a fraction of an instant, her heart leapt for joy.

Will was home!

But then her happiness whipped away, replaced by sheer terror.

That wasn't Will glaring at her from the front of the pack.

It was Sully Weatherspoon. And he looked angry.

Maggie dropped the washing with a loud scream and ran for the house.

She didn't even think about what she was doing. She just jumped up and ran, frightened in a way she couldn't have even explained.

Something in her, some primitive instinct, recognized danger and flooded her with fear, setting her legs and lungs in motion.

She screamed again as she sprinted toward the house, berating herself for not following Will's advice and carrying the derringer everywhere she went.

"Mama!" she cried, hurtling toward the house as fast as her legs would carry her. "Rose!"

But then, suddenly, she slammed to a stop fifty feet from the house to avoid crashing headlong into the heaving black wall that appeared before her.

Sully had cut her off, blocking her path with his muscular black stallion.

And now the other two men closed her in.

One, she realized with fresh terror, was Gibbs, the man who had tried to hit Will with brass knuckles in town—and who'd paid dearly for that offense. His mean eyes stared out from either side of a crooked nose on a face still discolored from cuts and bruising.

The other man she did not know and did not want to know. She just wanted to get away from them.

She took a step toward the house, trying to slip around Sully, but he moved his stallion, blocking her path again and sneered down at her.

Everything in Maggie wanted to scream again, but she reined in the urge, knowing—again instinctively, some animalistic part of her coming to life in this frightening situation—that to show fear now would be a terrible mistake. Fear only emboldened men like Sully Weatherspoon, amplifying their cruelty.

"Miss Dunne," Sully said. "It is indeed a pleasure to see you. I thought you were dead."

"My family is dead."

"So I heard. But I thought you'd burned alongside them. Pity."

"Pity that my family died?" she asked. "Or that I didn't burn with them?"

"Miss Dunne, your question wounds me. Why would I ever wish you harm?"

"Because I rejected your proposal."

Sully's face darkened at her words.

Maggie knew she should hold her tongue, knew that she was putting herself in danger here, but her temper leapt up, and before she could stop herself, she said, "And speaking of proposals, I am no longer Miss Dunne, as you insist in calling me. I am now Mrs. Bentley."

Sully sputtered with rage, his face going a dangerous crimson. "Bentley? As in Will Bentley? Did you marry Will Bentley?"

"That's right," Maggie said. "Will Bentley is my husband, and we're very happy."

"Where is he?" Sully demanded.

"Not here."

"Where did he go?"

"The Thicket, if you must know."

"The Thicket," Sully said and smiled suddenly.

Somehow, that smile frightened her more than his anger ever could have.

"Long way from here," Sully said. "Risky move, going down to the Thicket and leaving his pretty wife all alone. I mean, anything could happen to a woman out here. Anything at all. Nobody would even hear her scream."

Suddenly, Maggie was so terrified it was all she could do to keep her voice steady. "Well, he'll be home soon, so I really must be going, Mr. Weatherspoon. Good day."

She made a move to walk around him, but again he edged his stallion to one side, blocking her path. "You don't go anywhere until I'm finished with you, Mrs. Bentley. You thought you could snub me, you red-haired—"

"Boss," the man Maggie didn't know said. "Trouble coming."

"What is it, Chad?" Sully said, turning to follow the man's gaze.

Maggie looked past Sully to where Mama and Rose were hurrying this way, Rose holding a derringer in each hand, Mama pointing the shotgun straight at Sully.

"How dare you point a weapon at me?" Sully demanded.

Maggie, seeing her chance, ran around the stallion and hurried to Mama and Rose, who continued to point their weapons at the intruders.

"Sully Weatherspoon," Mama said, holding the double-barreled 10-gauge on him. "You leave my family alone, or I will send you straight to your reward."

Mama had never looked so much like Will, Maggie thought. Her eyes were hard and dangerous. Her voice was full of steel and rock steady, just like the hands gripping the shotgun.

"You can't kill all three of us," the man named Chad said, edging his horse away from Sully's.

"Maybe not, but at this range, you'll catch some lead, too, stranger. So will your horse. Now, get out of here, all three of you, before I give you both barrels."

"You can't tell me what to do," Sully said. "This is the new Texas. I'm going to be a big man. I'm going to run things, do you hear? Men like Will Bentley, we don't want his kind around here. Rabble-rousers, troublemakers, rebels."

"You mean men who will stand up to you," Maggie said.

Sully's eyes snapped in her direction, blazing with fury. She had no doubt now what he would have done if Mama and Rose hadn't come to her rescue.

"Like I said, this is the new Texas," Sully said. "You're going to wish you had accepted my proposal, Maggie. And you," he added, pointing at Rose. "You'd better pack your bags. Mr. Pew wants his wife back."

"Say his name again," Rose dared him, stepping closer and aiming down the short barrel of her derringer. "Say his name again, and I'll knock you out of that saddle, Sully."

Chad pulled a revolver from his belt. "We got 'em now, boss. That stupid girl stepped right into the path of that scattergun. The woman can't shoot without killing her, too."

Maggie's blood froze. Chad was right. Rose had stepped so close to Sully that Mama wouldn't dare to use the shotgun.

Sully grinned wickedly.

A shrill whistle sounded from across the field.

Everyone glanced in that direction and saw young Denny Smith standing at the edge of the property, holding a long-barreled musket that looked like it would have no trouble reaching across the hundred and fifty yards between them.

Coming through the trees behind him were his three towheaded brothers, each carrying a rifle of his own.

A second later, another whistle sounded from the other direction, and there was old Sam Waters and his son, both of them barefoot and wearing bib overalls... and holding rifles in their hands as well.

A third whistle sounded from the front behind them, and Maggie was thrilled to see yet another neighbor, Mrs. Johnson, walking this way, a baby on her hip and a revolver in her free hand.

Rose retreated, making the threat of Mama's shotgun deadlier than ever. She swung its barrel from Sully to the man named Chad, having realized just as Maggie had, that he was the most dangerous of the trio.

"Drop that revolver," Mama demanded.

Chad started to say something belligerent.

"Drop it or die!" Mama said, and everyone knew she meant it.

Chad, however, still hesitated, eyeing Mama with searing hatred.

"If she shoots," Maggie said, addressing Sully, "our neighbors will shoot, too."

"Drop the gun, Chad," Gibbs said, his voice lilting with fear.

"Yes," Sully said. "Drop the gun. These peasants are just stupid enough to shoot us."

Cursing, Chad lowered the hammer and leaned in his saddle and tossed the gun into the tall grass.

"This isn't over," Sully said, glaring at the women. "Not by a long shot. The authorities are going to hear about what you've done!"

CHAPTER 32

It was a good feeling, driving cattle up the lane toward home.

They had delivered half the cattle to a very happy Charles Forester, who whooped like a madman when they rode onto his ranch.

Forester wanted to know every detail of the trip. For the time being, however, Will shared the basics and told him he wanted to get his and Rufus's share of the herd home and check on his family.

They agreed to talk again later, and Forester said he'd get in touch with the cattle network and figure out the best way to drive all these cattle to market. Then the old rancher sent Fletcher and Hill along with Will and Rufus and the other hired men to drive the half-herd to Will's place.

Now, with the sun in his face, riding at the front of one hundred and fifty head of longhorn cattle, thanks to those they'd gathered on the return trip, Will felt like a conquering hero.

No one really won the Civil War, but the South had lost it. Disbanding and coming home had filled Will and the troopers of the 5th with the bitterness of failure.

This sensation, coming home after securing enough cattle to provide anything his family might need for a long, long time, was the exact opposite of defeat, and it filled him with triumph and optimism.

Maybe Forester was right. Maybe Will was a born cattleman.

But then the gates came into view—along with two bluebellies stationed there and what looked like a whole platoon of them camped around Will's home.

The sight gave him a jolt, and his first urge was to open fire.

Instead, he turned to Rufus. "Help the other men lead these cattle to pasture. I have to go check on my family."

"All right, Will," Rufus said. "But are you sure you don't want me to ride with you?"

"I appreciate it, Rufus, but no. Go take care of the herd."

"All right."

"And Rufus?"

"Yeah?"

"If shooting starts, get out of here. Tell the other men to ride, too."

Rufus shook his head. "We'll stand with you if it comes to fighting, Will."

"There's too many of them to fight. If shooting starts, run." Without waiting for a reply from his friend, Will broke away and rode toward the bluebellies.

The guards stepped forward, rifles at the ready.

Further back, closer to the house, men rose from where they'd been lounging and retrieved their rifles as well.

The guards halted Will and demanded to know his name and business.

"My name's Will Bentley. Where's my family?"

"It's him," the younger of the pair said in an alarmed voice. He lifted his rifle. "It's Will Bentley."

The other, older man wore corporal's stripes. "Lower your rifle, Stallworth. Mr. Bentley, I would ask that you peacefully surrender your arms and come with us, please."

"Am I under arrest?"

"You are being detained. For questioning."

"Why?" Will asked. But he knew. Sully had sicced them on him. Or maybe Pew.

Everything in him wanted to fight, but he surrendered his weapons and followed the men toward his home past other soldiers, who spread out, rifles in hand, watching him warily.

Reaching the house, Will dismounted.

A private stepped forward. "I'll take your horse for you."

"No, you won't," Will said, hitching Clyde to the post. "Nobody touches my horse."

"We'll do more than touch your horse, Johnny Reb," a burly, tough-looking sergeant said, stepping forward. "We'll take him. And your cattle, too. And we'll sell this ranch."

"On what grounds?"

"On grounds of you wore the gray," the hulking sergeant said and poked Will in the chest with a thick forefinger. The sergeant was obviously enjoying himself and showing off for the other men, whom he outranked. If this guy was in charge here, Will was in big trouble. "You fought against the Union. So you forfeited your right to property."

"Only thing I own is the clothes on my back," Will said.

"Lie all you want, Johnny Reb," the sergeant said, trying to goad him into a fight. "We're taking your ranch and your cattle and everything else you got, and there's nothing you can do about it."

The man poked him in the chest again. Harder this time.

The other troops stood by, ready to beat Will to a pulp if he stupidly rose to the bait, giving these bluebellies a reason to haul him off to a judge that would either lock him up or hang him.

So instead of smashing the sergeant's face with a hard right hand, Will simply smiled. "You don't seem to understand, friend. I don't own this place. Miss Dunne does. Check the deed. Just like she owns all the cattle we rounded up for her. And her father wore the blue. Died wearing it. With valor. You boys gonna rob the daughter of a brave Union soldier? An officer, no less? Sounds to me like you're fixing to get yourselves court-martialed. Maybe even hung, considering Mr. Dunne's friends in Washington."

Will didn't know if Mr. Dunne had had any friends in the North, but the rest of it was true enough, and it instantly had the intended effect.

The cocky sergeant backed down, looking worried. Then he turned his back on Will, grumbling for the other men to make sure Will didn't try anything before the captain came out.

A moment later, the farmhouse door opened, and through it strode a tall, gaunt bluebelly captain, the man who would decide Will Bentley's fate.

CHAPTER 33

Unlike these others, the officer looked like a real soldier.

He bowed politely to Mama, Maggie, and Rose, who appeared in the doorway now, looking surprisingly unruffled.

"I do thank you for the tea and conversation, Mrs. Bentley," the captain said. "And I thank you for the hospitality, Miss Dunne."

Will felt a thrill of admiration for his young wife, who'd been shrewd enough to hide their marriage from this man and his soldiers.

In Reconstruction Era Texas, nothing good could come of being married to Will Bentley.

Marvelously continuing the act, Maggie said, "Why, Captain Culp, here is Mr. Bentley now."

The officer swiveled, looked Will over, then excused himself politely, and came toward Will, walking in that strangely awkward, bowlegged way old cavalrymen so often did after years of never going on foot when there was a horse to ride.

"Will Bentley?" Culp said, studying his face.

"Yes, sir."

The captain surprised him then, sticking out his hand. "I'm Captain Alexander Culp, and I'd like to speak with you."

"Yes, sir," Will said, shaking the man's hand.

"Walk with me, son."

Will did as he was told.

The tough-looking soldier started to follow, but Culp dismissed him at once. "Sergeant Garrity, have these men police the area. I don't want any damage or trash left behind. These are good women here, and we will respect them and their property."

The big sergeant saluted his officer and started barking at the other soldiers.

"Now," Culp said to Will. "Let's talk."

"Yes, sir," Will said again, and they walked away from the others, Will listening, fury building within him as Culp explained why he was here.

The fury was not directed at Culp, who seemed like a reasonable man, but at the story he related.

"Sully Weatherspoon came to my office yesterday with quite a tale to tell," Culp said. "He said that he stopped to visit, and your mother, sister, and Miss Dunne threatened his life."

"Sir, Sully Weatherspoon has no business here."

"I understand that after speaking to your people, Mr. Bentley. Just between you and me, I have to say I enjoyed my conversation with them much more than my conversation with Sully Weatherspoon."

"Sully is a difficult person, sir."

Culp smiled faintly. "Yes, difficult. That is a diplomatic way to put it. While I congratulate you on your restraint, Mr. Bentley, I would ask that you speak openly with me now. That's why we're alone. I am new at this post, but I am determined to do my duty and further the mission, which is to stabilize the region, restore order, and deal with any problems that arise. I have no interest in getting rich along the way, and I have no old scores to settle. I merely wish to do my duty. Therefore, I need to know the truth. So I'll say it again, Mr. Bentley. Please speak openly with me."

"Sully Weatherspoon is a snake, sir."

Culp nodded. "That was my impression. When you're new, unfortunately, it can be difficult to sort out the truth. Especially when you have the reputation of an honest man. Tell me, Bentley, where have you been lately?"

"In the Thicket, sir."

Culp nodded. "Just as Weatherspoon said. What were you doing there?"

"Gathering cattle, sir."

Culp glanced at the herd working its way into the pasture. "So it would seem. Which directly contradicts what Weatherspoon told me. He claims that you're still fighting the war, that you and your neighbors are plotting an insurrection, and that you were campaigning in the Thicket, rounding up ex-confederates to come up here and fight alongside you."

Will boiled with anger. "Sully Weatherspoon is a liar. All I want to do is provide for my family. That's all I've ever wanted to do. Sully had no right to come here. I'd like to know what he was doing."

"According to Sully, he came here to bury the hatchet with you—something about a fight with one of his employees—but

JOHN DEACON

the women and some neighbors ran him off under threats of violence."

"More lies," Will said. "I wouldn't doubt they ran him off, but I guarantee he wasn't here to bury the hatchet… unless he meant to bury it in my head."

"I'll admit, he doesn't seem like one of Jesus's blessed peacemakers. He seems a lot closer to what you said—a snake, the sort who'll stir up trouble, looking for an edge, which I understand he had with my predecessor. Sully's father, it seems, is a man of some influence."

"He's rich."

"As is Mr. Pew."

"Is Pew in on this, too?"

"Not to my knowledge," Culp said. "I haven't even met the man. But I did hear you'd had trouble with him as well. Don't look so surprised Bentley. I've known your name for years. You and I are both cavalrymen, and I know a thing or two about your time on the battlefield. I will tell you this, off the record, of course. You have my respect."

"I appreciate that, sir."

"That respect led me to investigate you before coming here. Sheriff Rickert grudgingly told me about some trouble with Pew but insisted that he could handle the situation."

That news surprised Will. Even after their recent run-in, Rickert hadn't tried to rile up the bluebellies against him. Why not?

Maybe Rickert sensed that Culp was an honest man. Maybe he didn't want to seem incompetent. Or maybe Rickert was on the take from Pew and didn't want to share that money.

Whatever the case, it meant Rickert wasn't focused on Will's destruction the way Sully was. Perhaps, Rickert could even redeem himself. Only time would tell.

"What Rickert failed to tell me, however, was that Pew kidnapped your sister," Culp said, disgust clear on his face. "What sort of man would do such a thing?"

"A man who thinks he's above the law and everything else, including common decency."

"So it would seem. I sense, Mr. Bentley, that you are a good man, perhaps even an honorable man. But you are also a fighter. I know that to be true. And it sounds like you've been in a fair number of scraps since coming home not long ago."

"None of my choosing, sir."

Culp nodded and was silent for a time. They had come to the edge of the property. They stood in silence for a time, the only noise the gurgling of the creek before them.

"I wish the war was over," Culp said.

Will looked at him. "It is over, sir."

Culp shook his head. "Not for me, Bentley. Not for me. I have a wife at home. And two children, a girl of twelve and a seven-year-old son who barely knows me."

Culp turned to face him. They were of a height, and looked eye to eye; men, who, despite their vast differences, also shared similar bedrock. "I don't want to fight you, Bentley. I don't want to kill you. And I don't want to die here. I want to go home to my wife and children. I want my son to know me."

"Yes, sir."

"Since coming here, I haven't seen much of the troublesome Texan they talk about up north. Oh, there's Teal and his gang, and I would love to have that murderer's head stuffed and mounted over my fireplace, but mostly, folks around here seem like just that: folks, people trying to get by, people trying to put the past behind them, trying to take care of their families and live the type of life I want to live back in Ohio."

"Yes, sir. Us Texans can fight, but right now, we just want to get on with life. We're tired, sir. Bone tired."

"So it would seem."

For another several seconds, the only sound was the chuckling creek, its water running on and on and on.

Then Culp said, "But you're different, Bentley. You might be tired, but you are a warrior. I didn't just question Sully and Rickert and your family. I questioned your neighbors, too. Their stories line up with the women's, by the way, not with Sully's. Apparently, Weatherspoon was giving Miss Dunne a hard time before the guns came out."

Will clenched his fists, wanting to know more, and needing to do something about this. But now was not the time.

"Your neighbors don't just like you, Bentley. They admire you. And I believe that if you were to stir them up, as Weatherspoon accused you of doing, they would fight alongside you. I think you are the one person in this region who could convince them that they weren't so tired after all and that maybe some things are more important than getting on with life, that some things are truly worth fighting for."

Will said nothing.

"You are the one person who could prevent me from getting to know my son, Bentley. I don't believe a word of what Weatherspoon says, and I certainly won't allow him to trick or bribe me into doing his will."

Culp turned and looked Will in the eyes again. "But if you stir up any real trouble, Bentley, I will kill you."

There was no challenge in Culp's words, no eagerness, only sincerity. They didn't even feel like a threat. But he meant what he said, Will knew.

Culp glanced back toward the house. "Most of those men have never seen combat. You and the riders you could no doubt raise if you gave the call would wipe them out without breaking a sweat, let alone losing a man among you. But I have other weapons at my disposal."

"The traveling cavalry unit, sir?"

"That is correct. And they have seen combat. In fact, they have probably survived engagements against you. There are many of them, Bentley, and if I call, they will keep coming until you are dead and dust."

"I believe it, sir. And I'd rather not die."

"Good. We understand one another, then. I had hoped we would. I hope we can live in peace together. I hope I will go back to my family. And I hope that you and your family will build something here with all those cattle. It's a beautiful ranch that you bought here."

"I don't own the ranch, sir."

"Right," Culp said with a smile. "You are a shrewd man, Bentley. Not a snake like Weatherspoon, but smart. That was a wise move, putting the deed in 'Miss Dunne's name, just as it was a wise move not filing other public licenses."

Will smiled back at him, sensing no venom in the man. "I have no idea what you're talking about, sir."

"No, of course you don't," Culp said and stretched out his hand again.

Will shook it. "It's a pleasure to meet you, sir."

"Likewise, Bentley," Culp said. "I mean that with deepest

sincerity. You have a fine family here, a fine ranch, and now all these cattle. Your neighbors admire you and will look to you for guidance and, I think, help, if you live long enough to provide those things. Do us both a favor, young man, and stay out of trouble."

CHAPTER 34

It was a very happy reunion indeed once the soldiers left. The women were relieved that Captain Culp hadn't hauled Will off. They were overjoyed to have him home and ecstatic over the cattle he'd brought with him.

"Half of them belong to Rufus," he explained. "More than half, actually. But yeah, we did well, praise God. If we get these cattle to market and sell them for anything close to what they should go for, we'll be okay for a long time."

"You're not leaving again, are you?" Maggie asked.

"Not until I set things straight."

"What are you saying, son?" Mama asked. "Captain Culp seems like a reasonable enough man, but if you go stirring up trouble…"

He had explained his meeting with Culp, holding nothing back from his family.

"I can't just sit here hoping Sully will leave us alone," Will said. "He won't. Neither will Pew."

"But like Mama said," Rose jumped in, "Mr. Culp's warning was clear. We can't fight the bluebellies, too."

Will spread his hands. "I don't want to fight Culp. But I won't sit around waiting for Sully to set his next trap, either."

Maggie reached out and took his hand. "Will, don't feel the need to strike back on our account. We handled Sully and the others on our own. Well, with the help of our neighbors."

"Culp didn't say anything about others riding with Sully, but I'm not surprised. Sully wouldn't have the guts to come out here on his own. Who was with him?"

"Gibbs," Maggie said, "and some man named Chad."

Will nodded. "Chad Butler. He's the only one of the bunch who's a real threat. Man-to-man with a gun, I mean. He's not afraid, that's for sure. He's killed before, and folks say he's fast with that six-shooter of his."

Will had been thinking of Butler on the trip home, especially when, after making camp each night, he practiced Cullen Baker's quickdraw techniques, adapting them and making them his own, growing faster and faster with each session.

He reckoned Cullen Baker was right about the whole thing.

Folks had never much faced each other with pistols before the war. But they were doing it now. You heard about it from time to time, generally when a bad man like Butler gunned down someone in a saloon or bordello or over a card game gone bad.

It had the feel of something that was going to keep happening, something that was going to grow. And it wouldn't take folks long to figure out that getting a gun quickly into action was going to be a big part of whether they walked away from such a conflict or ended up with pennies on their eyes.

So Will was glad to be ahead of the curve and meant to make his draw as fast and smooth as he could before he had to use it.

Which could be any day now.

"I'm proud of how you ladies handled Sully and those others, and I'm thankful for our neighbors," Will said. "And don't worry. For as much as I want to punish Sully, I know I have to be smart."

"What are you fixing to do?" Mama asked.

"Well, I have to do something. We all agree that Sully won't just let things set, right?"

The women agreed.

"We need to set up defenses. Stay ready, keep a watch, talk to our neighbors. But if the cavalry taught me anything, it's to stay on the offensive whenever you can. Choose your battle. The time, the terrain. Everything you can control, control it. Then hit first, hit fast, and hit hard, ready to retreat and adapt, but always with a mind toward victory.

"Will, this isn't war," Maggie said.

"I know that, Maggie. And I have to keep it from becoming war. I have to do everything right. And I have to act quickly. Because men like Sully Weatherspoon are like mold. They work in the dark. I need to draw him out in the light, make this a fight between him and me. I can't stir folks up, go riding over to the Weatherspoon plantation, and burn it to the ground. Culp would call in the cavalry. I have to make this between Sully and me. Like a duel. Out in the open, out in the light, for all to see."

"Sully will never fight you man-to-man," Maggie said. "Not ever."

"It wouldn't seem that way," Will said, "but I have a plan that might trick him into doing just that."

CHAPTER 35

Whistling "Dixie," Will pushed through the batwings of the Red River Saloon.

It was a little before two in the afternoon, so the place hadn't cleared out yet.

Spotting the man he'd talked to after the fight with Gibbs, Will smiled and nodded.

The man lifted his beer in salute.

Will went to the bar.

Two dozen men stood there, most of them without drinks. With no money to spend, they probably came in just to talk.

One of them, Ted LaVoy, said, "Well, if it ain't Will Bentley. Ain't seen you since before the war."

Will shook his hand. "Good to see you, Ted."

"Hey, Larry!" Ted called across the bar. "Look what the cat dragged in!"

Old Larry Crenshaw put on a show, as he was wont to do,

dropping his mouth wide open as if Will were none other than Robert E. Lee. Then he came scampering over and shook Will's hand and set to jabbering.

The bartender, a man Will barely knew, came over and said his name and shook his hand and asked what he could get for him—on the house, he said with a wink, on account of Will putting Gibbs in his place.

That broke the place wide open.

The two o'clock crowd, many of whom had apparently been clearing out every day to avoid the three o'clock arrival of Gibbs and Sully, gathered around, slapping Will on the back and congratulating him and giving thanks.

Will's smile was genuine. He wasn't much for drinking, and he didn't need praise, but this was exactly the sort of reaction he'd been hoping for when he'd hatched a plan back on the ranch.

After helping settle the cattle and practicing his draw some more, Will had gone from neighbor to neighbor, thanking everyone who'd come out to help his family in his absence.

The neighbors were all happy to see him and happy to have helped—and happier still when Will gave each family a cow.

"There's more where that came from," he told each family, "and there should be even more later. You folks need something, you just let me know."

By the time he'd started his rounds, the plan was already forming in his mind. By the time he'd finished, after having witnessed his neighbors' grit and gratitude, the plan was basically complete.

"Boy oh boy, Will, we sure showed them bluebellies over at

Copper Run, didn't we?" asked Jake Stall, an infantryman Will had gotten to know during the war.

"We sure did, Jake," Will said. "Bartender, I want to buy a round for every man who wore the gray—and any man who wished he had."

The men roared with approval, and Will pulled out a wad of greenbacks. "We don't have any carpetbaggers in here, do we?"

A timid-looking fella at a table near the wall took this opportunity to slip out the door.

"Last one just vamoosed," someone laughed, and the rest of the bar joined in.

"Good," Will said. "I hate carpetbaggers. Been working up in Colorado, saving some money, so I can provide for my family. Well, I come home, find out this carpetbagger went and stole my farm."

The men growled and grumbled, several saying they'd lost their places, too. Someone suggested taking the carpetbagger who'd stolen Will's farm and running him out of town on rail. And putting the tar and feather to him for good measure.

"Wouldn't that be something?" Will said. "But no, I'll take care of him in time. Right now, I got a new place, and I'm too busy with cattle to worry about him."

"Cattle?" several men said at once.

"That's right, boys. Me, my friend Rufus, and old Charles Forester threw in together and rode down into the Thicket and gathered near on three hundred and fifty head. Some said not to bother. Said the bluebellies would just confiscate them. I say this is Texas. And Texas will rise again. But we gotta stand up like men for that to happen."

This riled them up. They set to whooping, and a few even let go with rebel yells.

"I sure wish I had known you was going down there," Dave Taylor said. "I would've ridden along and gave a hand."

"Me, too," one of the Farleigh boys said. Will didn't know which of the brothers he was, but he was a Farleigh, all right, and he was sincere.

Several others chimed in, saying they wished they'd gone, too.

"Well," Will said, taking his time, leaning back, and sipping his beer, making them wait a little, "things go as planned, I'm gonna need some help chasing out more cattle and pushing them up the trail. I'd be happy to pay you boys two dollars a day if you'd throw in with me."

"Two dollars a day!" Chet Elliot exclaimed. "I'd wrangle gators for two dollars a day!"

The room fairly erupted then, men excited by the prospect of making money, which was rare as hen's teeth in these parts.

Will bought another round, much to the glee of his friends, old and new, and said, "I just hope nothing gets in our way."

Everybody wanted to know what might stop Will and keep him from providing much needed work.

"You know how folks are," Will said. "They want to keep a man down."

"Bluebellies giving you trouble, Will?"

"Nah, that Captain Culp seems to be a fair enough fella. There's worse than bluebellies around these parts."

"Carpetbaggers!" men chorused.

"That's right," Will said. "But there's worse than carpetbaggers, too."

JOHN DEACON

"Scalawags!" they shouted.

"Traitors," Will said. "That's what they are. Men like Isaac Pew and Sully Weatherspoon. They're both giving me trouble. Big trouble."

Someone had heard about Will's sister and said something about it now, and all of them had heard about Will whupping Gibbs on the street.

"That ain't the half of it," Will said, and relayed the trouble Sully, Gibbs, and Butler had given his women.

The men roared with anger.

Will was not surprised. True Texans are nothing if not chivalrous to their women.

"Sully waited for me to leave, then snuck over like a fox sniffing around a henhouse. No way he'd face me man-to-man. Everybody knows he's yellow as a chicken yolk."

One of the men slapped the bar. "I seen him coming back from there. This was yesterday?"

"Yessir," Will said.

"I seen him, all right. I was coming out of the general store when Sully come riding up to the sheriff's office. Went running in there and started shouting at Rickert. I could hear him through the glass. Not the words, mind you, but the shouting. Then, Sully comes out of there and slams the door and rides off, looking fit to be tied."

"I run Rickert off about a week back," Will said. "But at least he had the guts to look me in the eye instead of creeping around, threatening women."

This got the other men going again. Several mentioned stories about Sully giving them or someone they knew a hard time. And everyone seemed to have something to say about Gibbs.

Will glanced at his watch. It was three o'clock on the dot.

Perfect.

And at that exact moment, the saloon door swung open.

CHAPTER 36

Will announced loudly, "Bartender, I'd like to buy another round for everyone who wore the gray or wished he had—but not him."

He turned in his chair and pointed across the room at Sully Weatherspoon, who stood just inside the door with Gibbs and Terry Tubbs, one of Sully's less impressive toadies.

Sully stared at Will with open hatred.

"Lieutenant Weatherspoon turned tail the first time the 5th took fire," Will declared loudly. "Ran out on his commission and had his daddy pay his way out of it. Now, he's a skalawag in the business of threatening women... because he's too afraid to stand up to a man."

"How dare you spread falsehoods about me, Will Bentley?" Sully demanded, his face turning purple with rage.

Will arched a brow. "You calling me a liar, Sully?"

"Yes, I am! You are a liar, and we aren't going to stand for—"

"Those are fighting words, Sully," Will said, standing and

pulling back his jacket to reveal his Colt, which sat in the holster he'd bought at the mercantile and practiced with in the alley outside before coming into the saloon.

Benny and Cullen Baker were right. It was much faster, whipping a gun out of a holster than it was dragging out one shoved through your belt.

Sully sputtered, his eyes locked on the revolver.

Behind him, Gibbs and Tubbs slipped from the saloon as silently as a pair of frightened barn cats.

"You men heard him," Will declared loudly. "Sully started it. He called me a liar. This is a fair fight between him and me. Whatever happens next, he had it coming."

Men nodded, clearing away, giving Will and Sully space.

"I…" Sully said, and whatever he'd been going to say seemed to stick in his throat. His eyes swelled, and all the color drained from his face.

He looked for his friends and gave a little start when he realized that Gibbs and Tubbs had both abandoned him.

"You're lucky," Sully said, sounding like a petulant child. "I don't have a firearm. Otherwise, I'd teach you a lesson."

Several men moved forward at once, drawing their revolvers and offering them to Sully butt-first.

"No, no," Sully said, taking a step backward. "I never use another man's weapon."

"How come you ain't got a gun, Sully?" someone demanded. "You always got a gun."

One of the men reached over, snagged Sully's coat, and pulled it aside.

And there, on his hip, was the revolver he'd denied having.

Will wanted to draw his own weapon and kill the man

who'd threatened his wife and family, the same man who'd sent the bluebellies, hoping for Will's execution. But if he did, Rickert or Culp would apprehend him, and some Reconstruction judge would find him guilty of murder and hang him.

He needed Sully to draw first. That was why he'd come here, his only hope at taking care of this without causing himself bigger troubles.

"Come on, you coward," Will said. "You're man enough to frighten women and man enough to call me a liar. Now, you'd better be man enough to fight me. On three…"

Sully's eyes swelled, and he took another step backward.

"One," Will said, and smiled at his enemy. "Two…"

"No!" Sully cried, his voice high and sharp with fear, and he dove from the bar.

"You'd best be careful, Will," Jake Stall said. "You unmanned him publicly. He'll try to kill you for this."

"Nah," Will said. "Sully doesn't have the guts."

But inwardly, he knew Jake was right. Sully would likely try to kill him for this.

That, or tuck tail and leave town.

Either of those things would suit Will just fine.

CHAPTER 37

Sully Weatherspoon had never been so angry in all his life. Not just at Will Bentley but also at his father, who had been treating him like a child ever since the incident at the saloon several days earlier.

There was other anger, deeper within him, as well; anger he refused to consider at any great length; anger at himself for not facing Will Bentley; anger at what some part of him knew to be cowardice.

Sully stood now in his father's office, trembling with impotent rage.

"Your error is costing us dearly," his father said, pacing back and forth behind his big desk. "Will Bentley has been coming into town every day, dragging our name through the mud. People see me passing by, they cover their mouths and laugh. I am not a laughingstock, Sully!"

"No, sir," Sully said but wanted, out of sheer spite, to point out that his father was, indeed, a laughingstock. He'd admitted to just that.

But Sully said no such thing because his father's other side was showing now. Not the aristocratic plantation owner or the pillar of the community, who had welcomed the Reconstructionists, or even the hard-nosed businessman, but that other side, the side only Sully knew.

The cold-blooded killer.

"What are we going to do, Father? Shoot him down in the street?"

"No, we're not going to gun him down in plain sight. He's well-liked. Every time he comes to town, folks mob him. He throws his money around and talks about cattle and Texas rising again. You'd think he was running for mayor."

His father shook his head with irritation and continued to pace back and forth.

"So what do we do?" Sully asked.

"We strike from cover. We can't let folks know it was us."

His father stopped pacing, lifted a painting from the wall, and opened the safe hidden there, then came back out with a stack of bills.

"Want me to pay off the bluebellies?" Sully asked, doing his best to conceal his fear.

"No, I do not. He hasn't troubled us since you paid him, but that didn't help your cousin, did it?"

"No, sir."

"I am beginning to suspect that Culp isn't for sale. Which complicates things. If I send enough money to a man I know in the North, I could probably have Culp replaced, but that would take time we don't have and money I'd rather not spend."

Sully's father squeezed his hand into a fist, crinkling the crisp greenbacks. "No, there is a more direct, affordable way to handle this without bringing suspicion on ourselves. Will Bentley had stirred these idiots up. They're ready for a fight. If he dies, and we're involved in any way, they'll lynch us in the town square."

Sully tugged at his collar. He could almost feel the noose squeezing his throat.

"Take this," his father said, handing him the bills. "Here's what I want you to do."

As Sully listened, a smile crept onto his face.

It was such a simple, brutally effective plan, it was bound to work. Why hadn't he thought of it himself?

"I'll take care of it right away," he promised and started for the door.

"One more thing, Sully," his father said, and Sully turned back around to see hard eyes staring directly at him, almost through him. "Make sure every penny goes to the man I want you to hire. Do you understand?"

Something in Sully crumbled. How much did his father know?

"Yes, Father," he said and went out the door, feeling uneasy.

The way the man had looked at him, he almost seemed ready to kill Sully, too.

But even these troubling notions couldn't hold down Sully's spirits, which again lifted with optimism and satisfaction. This simple, beautiful, merciless plan was certain to work.

Will Bentley was a dead man!

CHAPTER 38

"Count me in, Will," Jake Stall said. "I'll ride with you."

"Me, too," Ted LaVoy said. "I never did much roping, but I'm sure I can learn."

"We'll all be learning on the job," Will said. "And every time we do a gather or drive them to market, we'll get better at it."

The men at the bar nodded. They'd really come to life since Will had started coming into the Red River Saloon every day.

He now had plenty of men to do a big gather in the Thicket, and plenty who were ready to brave the Chisholm Trail.

But Will had more business in here than just drumming up a crew. Every day, he reminded them of Sully's cowardice, his dereliction of duty in the war, the things he'd tried to do to Will, and the way he and Gibbs had run roughshod over these men themselves.

He also reminded them of how the Weatherspoons had embraced the Reconstructionists and how pretending to support the Union while still keeping so-called servants in a state that could only be called slavery.

"They're liars," Will would say, pausing to look around at the men nodding in agreement. "Liars and cowards, cheats and thieves and traitors."

He spoke similarly of Isaac Pew, who remained a concern. The crazy old man wouldn't forget what Will had done to him. Sooner or later, he would realize that Rickert couldn't solve the problem for him. Then he'd move on to something else.

When he did, Will would be ready for him.

"What about the raiders down there in the Thicket?" Tim Warren asked. "I hear there's a bunch of them. You think they'll give you any trouble?"

Will spread his hands. "Most of the men down there are just good old boys who wore the gray. The Reconstructionists stole their farms and their stock. They got nothing left. And some of them, maybe even most, have had run-ins with law. Probably just for having defended Texas. Now, they're out in the swamps, laying low, waiting for this to blow over. We ran into one bunch last time, and they were nice as anything. Even escorted us back out."

"What about Teal's gang?" someone asked.

"Teal's a different story," Will said. "We run into his gang, we'll have to fight our way out of there. They're a bunch of murdering savages."

"I was here the day they came and robbed the bank," Dale Vance said. "Rode into town, whooping and shooting and—"

The saloon door swung open.

Will, who always positioned himself now with his back to

the wall, saw who it was, saw the expression on his face, and knew that big trouble had finally arrived.

He stood to face the newcomer.

"Heard you been running your mouth about me, Bentley," Chad Butler said through his teeth. He stood there, framed in the doorway, a shadowy figure thanks to the afternoon light behind him, a tendril of pale smoke rising from the thin black cigar clamped in his sneer.

Butler's hand hovered at his side, clearly ready to seize the butt of the Colt shoved through his belt.

"Actually, Butler," Will said, "I haven't bothered to say much about you. What's to say? You're just a hired gun. And a failed one at that. First you came out to my neck of the woods with Rickert, and I ran you off. Then you came back out with Sully, and the women scared you off. I don't see any reason to even mention you."

The other men chuckled—but also cleared the way. They could all see what was coming.

"Want us to throw him out of here, Will?" Jake asked.

"No, no," Will said. "Seems like I hurt his feelings, telling the truth. I'll let him sass me a little. Then I'll pat him on the head and send him home. Might help him to feel like a real man."

"I'm surprised to hear you running your mouth," Butler said. "You ain't got your scattergun today."

Will had his own hand close to his Colt. "Get out of here, Butler. Everybody knows you don't have the guts to face me man-to-man."

Of course, Will knew Chad Butler had enough guts to use his gun. And Will was ready for it. He just wanted to push him into drawing first.

Butler spat the smoking cigar on the floor. "I'll show you who's got guts," Butler said, and grabbed for his gun.

Butler was fast.

Will had known he would be. That was part of why he'd practiced his own draw every day since learning Cullen Baker's tricks, wanting to be ready for this moment.

Which he was.

Butler yanked his weapon free and was just bringing it to bear when Will shot him through the chest, drew back the hammer, and shot him again, lower this time, punching a hole in his miserable guts.

Butler's gun went off and smashed a mug on the bar.

Then he was down on the ground, his Colt forgotten. He hitched around, making sounds for a while, the way men do sometimes when they're hit hard and don't want to die.

Then Butler did just that, giving up the ghost, and lay there with eyes open and empty, staring up from the floor beside his still smoldering cigar, which continued to add to the haze of gun smoke now hanging heavily in the air until Will stepped over and ground the cigar beneath his boot, extinguishing for good, just as he had its owner.

A moment later, the saloon doors opened again, and Sheriff Rickert stepped inside, gun drawn. Rickert glanced at Butler, dead on the floor, then pointed his gun at Will.

"Put down your gun, Will," Sheriff Rickert said. "You're under arrest."

The men exploded with fury, rallying around Will, and closed in on Rickert, declaring Will's innocence and demanding justice.

They all told it the same way. Butler had come in here

hunting trouble. Will had stood up to him. And Butler had drawn first.

Drawn first and died for his mistake.

A fair fight all the way around.

As the men crowded around him, getting angrier with each passing second, Rickert's face got paler and paler. He put away his gun and raised his palms, trying to calm the angry men, understanding that they would tear him limb from limb if he tried to jail Will.

"All right, all right," Rickert said. "You men settle down. I understand now. How was I supposed to know what happened? I just heard the gunshots and come running. Saw Butler on the ground and Will standing there with a gun in his hand. I didn't know it was a fair fight."

The men eased up then, giving Rickert some space.

The sheriff shook his head, looking from Butler to Will. "I knew Butler was a hothead, and I knew he didn't like you, but I didn't think it would come to this."

"He didn't come in here because he didn't like me," Will said. "He came in here because somebody paid him to assassinate me."

"Assassinate you?" Sheriff Rickert said incredulously. "Who would pay to have you killed."

"You know exactly who paid him to kill me, Rickert." Will knew exactly who had hired Butler. But that didn't stop him from saying, "Isaac Pew."

CHAPTER 39

Again, Sully found himself across the desk from his father, who paced back and forth while Sully sat.

"He said there was no reason for his troops to get involved," Sully reported. "Said the sheriff already has everything under control."

Sully's father looked disgusted. "That settles it, then. Captain Culp is not our man. Once we've settled things with Bentley, I'll get to work on having him replaced."

"I can't believe Rickert actually arrested Mr. Pew," Sully said.

"The old fool brought it on himself. He's so used to having his way, he's lost his edge. Besides, he wouldn't stop pestering Rickert about Bentley. Rickert's probably happy to have the old man out of his hair."

"For now," Sully said, "but we'll see how happy Rickert is after Mr. Pew pays off the judge and gets free again. He'll have Rickert's scalp."

235

Sully's father shook his head and turned his look of disgust on Sully. "Pay off the judge? With what?"

"With money, of course."

"Money? What money? Didn't you listen to a word I said? The minute they hauled Pew off, his own people robbed him blind, and someone set his house on fire. His own people turned on him."

"The ungrateful scoundrels," Sully said.

"What reason did those people have to be grateful? Pew treated them worse than you treat our slaves. They saw their opportunity and seized it. That's human nature. Now, Pew is ruined."

"I don't understand why Will Bentley gave Rickert Pew's name," Sully said. "He had to know it was us."

His father stopped pacing and showed him half a smile. "Ah, finally, you're thinking. That's the piece that makes no sense. You're right, of course. Bentley's smart enough to know we sent Butler. So why not accuse us? What's Bentley up to? What is he planning?"

"He's trying to ruin our name."

"Yes, and he's doing a good job. But there has to be more to it than that. Everything's so efficient, so calculated. Like this move with Pew, accusing him instead of us, mere moments after the fight. He was ready for us. Ready for Butler or someone like him. And he had already thought things through, already knew what he would say to the sheriff, whom he would accuse, all of it. We're up against a shrewd opponent, son, a very dangerous man."

"You give him too much credit, Father. Will Bentley used to

pick cotton for us. He's just a peasant. A pig farmer who never had two pennies to rub together."

Sully's father stared at him, studying him and not seeming to like what he saw. "Where did I go wrong with you? Never mind. But don't underestimate Bentley. He's a very dangerous man indeed, and you underestimate him at your peril. Which leaves us only one choice."

Sully's father again removed the painting from the wall, opened the safe, and pulled out money. More this time. Much more.

Sully sat up straighter, interested by the money and by whatever his father had in mind. Sully had no clue what that might be, since Butler was dead and Culp had proven useless.

"Call Gibbs and three other men who can fight. Saddle up and bring your rifles. You ride tonight."

Sully's guts turned to water. He shot to his feet. "Sir, we can't attack Bentley. He'll be ready for us. You don't understand. He's—"

"Shut up, coward!" Mr. Weatherspoon shouted with such fury that Sully dropped once more into his seat. "Do you think I'm stupid?"

"No, sir."

"This is our real weapon," Sully's father said, patting the stacked greenbacks. "Money. But like any weapon, you must aim it carefully to ensure maximum damage. I wouldn't trust you to finish the job. But I will trust you to deliver this money to the one man who can. Where you're going, however, you'll need Gibbs and the others to protect you along the way."

CHAPTER 40

The next week was quiet for Will and Maggie. Quiet but not calm, because their lives crackled with expectation.

Attack was imminent. They could both feel it, as could Mama and Rose and Rufus.

Candy, who had quit her job with the Weatherspoons and moved into the bunkhouse after a hurried marriage to Rufus, said things on the plantation had also been tense and quiet.

Mr. Weatherspoon had been staying mostly behind closed doors, and Sully had disappeared altogether.

No one seemed to know where he'd gone.

"Something's cooking over there," Candy said. "I don't know what it is, but it ain't good."

Will had seen no sign of Sully in town. Not that Will had gone in much since the fight with Butler.

When he had visited, he kept his eyes open, took care of the day's business, and didn't loiter.

Sully wouldn't send another man like Butler to face him

again. Next time, Sully would either attack with overwhelming force or maybe have somebody shoot him in the back.

So Will was careful, during his few trips to town, to avoid any pattern that might allow someone to arrange such a trap, and he avoided the saloon other than the day he stopped in and hired three men—Jake Stahl, Ted LaVoy, and the young but tough Farley Farleigh—to come out to the ranch.

Officially, they were hands, and they did help manage the longhorns, but everyone knew why he'd hired three fighting men.

If Sully came out here with a pack of shooters, Will would be ready for him.

Jake, Ted, and Farley spent their days around the ranch but stayed over at Maggie's old bunkhouse, where they enjoyed suppers prepared by the new Mrs. Twill, who had cooked for the Weatherspoons before being liberated by Rufus and the promise of his cattle money.

Will had also talked again to his neighbors and worked out a plan that would help protect him without putting them at any real risk.

As always, they were happy to help.

Except Braintree, of course. Whenever he saw Will, the carpetbagger quickly looked the other way and stumped inside as fast as his bad leg could carry him.

The weather shifted, going from cool to hot, leapfrogging the spring weather every Texan cherishes.

They'd had just enough rain to germinate the crops, which broke through the dark, rich soil, unperturbed by the human drama brewing.

JOHN DEACON

The night trouble finally came, Will and Maggie made love then lounged in the darkness of their room, talking.

They had opened a window, hoping for a breeze, but the air was hot and listless. Through it, they heard the lowing of the herd, which Jake was currently watching over, and which Will had been recently keeping in the pasture closest to the house. He was edgy. Not impatient, exactly—he knew how to wait—but eager for action. Yearning for it, in fact, now that things had been set in motion.

"I can't believe the judge actually gave Pew life in prison," Maggie said.

"I can. Pew had probably been paying him off for years. But it sounds like Pew's employees—his former slaves, most of them—robbed him blind as soon as they hauled him off to jail. With no money to bribe the judge, Pew finally received justice."

"Is it justice, though, Will? Pew didn't hire Butler. Sully did. You said you were certain of that."

"Yeah, either Sully or his daddy. But what does that matter? What's the sentence for kidnapping a woman, keeping her prisoner for a month, and trying to force her to marry you? What's the sentence for bribing a judge? What are the sentences for all the other things he's been getting away with? Pew is a wicked man who's been doing terrible things to people since before we were born. The only thing that had been keeping him safe was money. Now, his money's gone, and he's no longer above the law. Justice was served."

"You're right," Maggie said. "I've been wondering, though. Why did you tell Rickert it was Pew?"

"Because Pew was a threat. I was tired of keeping my eyes on Sully and having to keep looking back over my shoulder, wondering if Pew was sending someone to shoot me in the back."

"But still, Sully's more dangerous than Pew. You said so yourself."

"Far more dangerous. At least his father is. But accusing them wouldn't have done any good. They're heavily connected with the Reconstructionists. Rickert never would have arrested them, and the judge would have dismissed their case, anyway. Meanwhile, nobody likes Pew. They would take his money to a point, but he's not slick like Weatherspoon. Things worked out perfectly."

"Yes, I suppose they did, praise God," Maggie said. "I do wish this was all over. I just want to get on with our lives together."

He kissed her gently. "We are getting on with our lives."

"You know what I mean, Will."

"Yeah, I do. And I look forward to that, too. But life's full of trouble. You can't sit around waiting for it to be over. You gotta keep right on living. Otherwise, life will pass you by. You'll waste it worrying."

"I suppose."

They lay there for a while, Maggie twirling her fingertips in his chest hair. They talked idly from time to time but mostly just enjoyed being close to each other.

Then, a gunshot split the night.

It came from a distance, miles to the south.

Will sat up, listening hard.

"What is it?" Maggie asked.

The gun fired again.

Will was up and moving.

"What is it?"

"Wait," Will whispered, listening.

And there it was, the third shot.

"They're coming for us, Maggie. Wake Mama and Rose. I gotta get outside and warn the men."

"Who's coming for us?"

"I don't know. But that was the sign us neighbors agreed on. Three shots means somebody's coming. Whoever it is, they're coming from the south."

They lit a lamp and got dressed in a hurry.

Pulling on his cavalry boot, Will confessed, "I was hoping they wouldn't come from the south."

"Why's that?"

"I don't want to scare you. I just want you to be ready is all."

"What is it, Will? Just tell me."

"If they were coming from town, they'd approach from the west. But whoever this is, they're coming from the south, from the direction of…"

Maggie's eyes were bright with fear, but her voice was steady. "The Thicket."

"That's right, Maggie. I think that's where Sully's been. I think Teal's coming back."

CHAPTER 41

Will told the night guard, Jake Stall, what was happening.

Jake pounded off to alert the men sleeping in the Dunnes' bunkhouse, but they met him halfway. Farley had heard the gunshots, awakened Ted, and they'd come running.

Will woke Rufus and Candy.

By this time, Will's family had come outside, too. The women looked worried, but each carried a firearm. Maggie had his Dragoon. Rose had the pepperbox. Mama toted her scattergun.

Will likewise had his cut-down ten-gauge slung over his shoulder. Across his chest, the bandolier held fifty rounds of double-ought buckshot. His Colt hung on one hip. The fourteen-inch Confederate Bowie hung on the other. He gripped his Spencer rifle. Slung over his other shoulder was the Blakeslee box with its heavy cargo of thirteen quick-load magazines, each carrying seven .56-.56 cartridges.

"I don't know who's coming," Will told everyone. "If it's the bluebellies, do not fight. I'll try to talk my way out of it. But no matter what happens, do not fight. There are too many of them."

The men grumbled.

Will didn't let them build any steam. "But I don't think it's the bluebellies. I think it's Teal. I think Sully Weatherspoon went down there and hired him to do his dirty work."

The men nodded.

"They're coming from the south," Rufus said. "Could be Teal."

"Whoever it is," Jake said, "he's gonna wish he'd stayed away."

"If it's Teal, he'll bring a lot of men with him," Will said. "He had eighteen riders, last I heard. I don't expect you men to stand beside me. Not with these odds."

"You think I'm gonna run, you got another thing coming," Farley said. Farley was too young to have fought in the war, but Will could tell he had grit.

"I'll stand," Ted said.

"We're partners," Rufus said. "Free men facing the world together. I'm not going anywhere."

"You know I'll fight," Jake said and spat on the ground for emphasis. "You and me made it through worse scrapes than this in the war, and by gum, we're gonna make it through this one, too."

Will was pretty sure they'd never faced odds this long, but now was not the time to debate, so he merely thanked the men for standing with him then said, "Whoever it is, they'll be here soon. If it's Teal, we'll have to fight hard and smart. I'm gonna saddle Clyde and get behind the barn, close to the pasture."

The men glanced in that direction. The cattle, sensing their tension, were up and moving around and getting louder with every second.

"You men spread out. Find cover and set up at different angles. Someone over yonder behind that big oak. Somebody over on the other side, down in the creek close to Braintree's place. And somebody out closer to the gate. Stay behind that big rock where they won't see you. They'll ride right past you. Nobody shoot until they hear my shot. Then we'll hit them from all sides. It isn't much of a plan, but it's our best chance. You all shoot straight, they might panic and ride out of here. They're mercenaries, not freedom fighters.

The men nodded, spoke briefly among themselves, and moved off into the darkness to take up their various positions.

Will turned to the women. "I'd tell you to ride off, but Teal's an old trooper and might have outriders scouting the flanks. I don't want you getting shot or captured."

"We'll fight with you," Maggie said.

"No," Will said. "These men are killers. You ladies hole up until this is over."

Maggie shook her head. "You're my husband, Will. I'm going to fight at your side."

"No," he said, and this time, his voice was iron.

Maggie opened her mouth to say something but stayed silent.

"Hide in the bunkhouse," he told them. "No one will expect you to be there. And if it's Teal, well, he didn't burn the Dunne's bunkhouse. But if he wipes us out and does find you in there, fight with everything you've got. Teal isn't known for mercy."

Mama lifted her shotgun. "First one through the door gets both barrels."

"One'll do the job, Mama," Will said. "Give him the left and save the right barrel for the next one."

"Share and share alike," Mama said with a gritty smile. "Come on, ladies. Son, if it comes to fighting, kill these men. All of them. We'll be praying for you."

Will nodded.

There was no time for drawn-out goodbyes.

Maggie darted in, gave him a quick kiss, and followed the other women toward the bunkhouse.

Will saddled Clyde, secured the Blakeslee box, and mounted up, gripping the Spencer rifle. The cut-down messenger gun was still slung over his other shoulder.

"Well, Clyde, we're in for it now. You ready for some action?"

The big horse tossed his head, ready as always.

Will rode to the northeast corner of the barn, where he could keep an eye on the space in front of the house without exposing himself to riders coming from the south.

A short distance away, his house was completely dark. To the raiders, it would look like everyone was still asleep.

Between there and here, the cattle crowded the gate, making a lot of noise, restless, the men's tension having riled them up.

Will peered out toward the lane. His eyes had adapted to the night, and there was enough of a moon out that he could see clearly all the way to the hedgerow, but beyond those trees, all was darkness.

He wasn't happy with this plan. As a veteran cavalryman, he preferred to stay on the offensive. Depending on how many men were coming, however, Will and his friends might be able to drive them back.

But if Teal had his whole outfit...

Well, if that was the case, Will and his friends would just have to fight their hardest and go to their graves knowing they'd died fighting like men.

He only hoped, if that happened, that Teal would search the house, find it empty, and assume the women had fled. Which seemed likely.

Will did not fear death and wasted no time worrying, but when he spotted a double column of torches trotting up the lane and he estimated their count, he nodded grimly to himself.

Death, then.

There was a flicker of regret, mostly to do with Maggie and the future they might have shared, but he squashed it immediately, recognizing all such sentiment as weakness... especially in a moment like this.

A moment where Will Bentley must become a killing machine. If not to survive then to punish those who meant to kill him.

It was Teal, all right.

Who else could summon so many night riders?

Twenty-three by Will's count.

Twenty-three to five.

Long odds indeed.

So be it.

A familiar calm settled over him, tinged in red. He hadn't felt this in a long time, not since his last full-scale battle.

The killing calm.

He welcomed it like the old friend it was and felt the thrill of impending action as two columns of men rode onto the property and massed themselves in front of the house, their faces weird and savage and indistinct in the flickering torchlight, less like the faces of men and more akin to crude masks carved by some primitive tribe that worshipped gods of blood and fire.

One of these men must be Teal.

Will scanned their faces, hoping to kill the leader first.

Was that Teal? He was the right age but clean-shaven and bigger than Will would have expected, based on Benny's description.

No. Not Teal.

At least, he didn't think so.

But now, one rider separated himself from the pack and rode forward to face Will's empty house, his eyes and nasty smile gleaming in the torchlight.

Again, not Teal.

It was Sully Weatherspoon.

CHAPTER 42

Sully smiled up at the darkened home and shouted, "Will Bentley! Come out here, you coward!"

Sully let a giggle slip.

It gave him a special thrill using that word against Will Bentley.

Coward.

Because, although Sully's courage had previously been called into question, who had ridden all the way to the Thicket, employed these bloodthirsty raiders, and led them here?

Sully, that's who.

And now, he had moved out in front of them to let Will Bentley know how it was going to be.

Not Teal, Sully.

Were those the actions of a coward?

Certainly not!

In fact, if anyone was being cowardly at this moment, it was

Teal. Despite his reputation, gruff mannerisms, and tough talk, Teal remained at the center of his men, as if frightened to put himself in danger.

Well, Sully was not afraid. He was triumphant.

He could not wait to tell Father all about this glorious night.

This would wipe out all Father's doubts and show him once and for all that Sully was a worthy heir to his plantation, fortune, and legacy.

Would even Father dare to do what Sully was doing now?

No. No, he would not. Alistair Weatherspoon would never put himself at such risk.

Drunk with glee, Sully stifled another giggle.

Then, drawing himself straight again, he shouted once more, "Will Bentley, come out here, you coward! If you surrender yourself, we will spare your family. But if you don't, or if you fire a shot, everyone dies. And I mean *everyone*. We'll hunt them all down and kill every last one of them!"

It was a lie, of course.

Sully would kill them even if Will Bentley surrendered.

Killing the woman who'd spawned Will Bentley would be a pleasure. And with Pew now powerless, Rose Bentley was of no use to Sully. She might, however, seem downright useful to Teal's men, who would have plenty of fun with her before putting a bullet through her brain.

The only one Sully would preserve—temporarily—was Maggie. Because he still had uses for her. Oh yes. He would use her again and again until he grew tired of it. Then he would dispose of her himself.

He'd given Teal and the others clear orders concerning Maggie. No one was to kill the red-haired woman. Instead, they were to bring her directly to him, where her pitiful begging would be music to his ears.

"Let's go, Bentley! Surrender yourself now, and you can still save the women. Come on! Time's almost up! What are you, a coward?"

CHAPTER 43

Will was still scanning the men when Sully gave his ultimatum.

Beneath him, Clyde was steady as always. Behind him, the cattle were growing even more restless. Blatting with fear, eyes rolling, they pressed against the gate, wanting to flee.

Sully's threat was chilling. He knew Will's family was here and was making sure Will understood that he would kill them all.

Will didn't doubt him for a second. A cruel, cowardly man like Sully, once he got the upper hand, would do terrible things.

Like murdering innocent women.

Will had formed the best plan possible, maximizing their fighting chances and hiding the women away from the structure Teal was most likely to burn.

But if Will fought now, if he so much as fired a warning shot, Sully would make a point of finding and butchering Mama, Rose, and Maggie.

THE PROVIDER

Will had been ready to fight, ready to die.

But he saw no way to beat these men. He needed more soldiers on his side and wished he had a strong force to charge with him straight into the fray.

He was alone, though. Yes, the other men would fire from their positions and undoubtedly kill some of Teal's raiders, but Will's friends would all die eventually.

Will, Rufus, Jake, Ted, Farley...

And, Will now understood, the women would die as well.

Then the raiders would plunder Will's home, burn it to the ground, and steal his cattle.

All because of Sully. All because, when you got right down to it, a cotton-picking day laborer named Will Bentley hadn't allowed the spoiled son of a plantation owner to beat him to a pulp with his riding crop.

"Be brave, Bentley!" Sully shouted. "This is between you and me, not the women. Come out here, or they all die, too!"

It was not an idle threat, Will knew. Sully had no soul, and Teal would spare no one. The marauder had already proven that by murdering Maggie's family and countless others, both in the war and after.

Would Sully honor the deal, though? If Will surrendered himself, would Sully really allow the others to live?

Will hoped so.

Because there was no other way. This force was too big, too bloodthirsty.

Will had to sacrifice himself. There was no other way to save his friends and loved ones.

"Last chance to save your family, Bentley!" Sully shouted.

"Show yourself now or they all die! I'll give you to the count of three. One…"

CHAPTER 44

When Sully Weatherspoon started talking, Maggie went to the window of the darkened bunkhouse, stared out at the cluster of torch-bearing men in front of her home, and shuddered with revulsion.

It was like remembering something she had never actually experienced, like seeing the moment before Mother and Maggie's two brothers had been murdered.

Behind this shudder, however, came not weakness but anger.

Rage, in fact.

How dare Sully bring Teal and his killers here?

She hated them and prayed for their utter destruction.

Now, Sully was threatening Will, telling him to step forward and surrender himself or they would kill everyone else, too.

Maggie ran to the door.

"What are you doing?" Rose asked, her voice full of panic.

"I'm going out."

"No," Mama said. "Will said—"

"Didn't you hear Sully?" Maggie said. "You know Will. If I don't go out there, he'll sacrifice himself to save us. I can't let him do that. I'd rather die fighting alongside my husband."

Gripping the big Dragoon in one hand, Maggie opened the bunkhouse door and slipped into the shadows outside.

The cattle were going crazy now, banging into the fence and making a racket.

Where was Will?

Her eyes searched the darkness behind the barn.

There!

She saw him sitting on Clyde, peering out at the raiders, a glint of moonlight on his rifle barrel.

How she loved him. She had to get to him before he fell for Sully's lies.

But then Sully counted to three and shouted, "All right, Bentley, if you're too much of a coward to save your family—"

And Will called from the darkness, "I'm here."

No! Maggie couldn't let Will sacrifice himself.

"You win, Sully," Will said, starting to come forward. "I'll do it. I—"

Whatever Will had been going to say vanished when Maggie pointed the big Dragoon in the direction of Teal's raiders, hauled back on the hammer, and pulled the trigger.

CHAPTER 45

Will had just been coming out from behind the barn when someone near the bunkhouse fired a shot.

Instinctively, he jerked back behind cover, but by the big bellow of the gun, Will knew it was the Dragoon.

Maggie was out here!

Then everything exploded, two dozen guns firing at once.

Bullets slammed into the corner of the barn, showering him in splinters.

"Maggie!" he shouted. "Take cover!"

He slid off Clyde, walked the horse back, and tethered him to the rail away from the shooting. Then he got onto his belly and crawled back over to the corner, where he opened fire on the enemy, who seemed to be firing in all directions now as Will's friends hidden in the darkness also opened fire.

Sully and Teal had expected to find Bentley asleep in a farmhouse with three women. Easy pickings in their minds.

But now, they found themselves pinned between five

snipers and one of the very women they had discounted, who fired again and again from somewhere beyond the bunkhouse, hopefully behind cover.

Will unseated one raider, fired into the mass, hit another… then had scooted back around the barn when bullets started chewing up the ground where he'd been lying.

They'd spotted his muzzle flash.

Soon, they'd be coming around the other side of the barn, trying to get at him from behind.

But for now, most of them were still out there in the open, firing in all directions.

Meanwhile, the cattle, wild with fear, pressed into each other, pushing into the gate, bawling with terror, wanting to run, desperate to escape…

That's it! Will thought.

Shoving the Spencer into its boot, he leapt atop Clyde and charged to the gate.

Teal's men opened up on him.

A bullet seared across his back, laying him open in a line of hot fire as if he'd taken a lash from a bullwhip.

Ignoring the pain, he leaned down and threw the latch.

An instant later, the gate banged open, and a river of terrified cattle rushed forward—and straight toward Teal and his men.

Swinging the stubby ten-gauge into his right hand, Will peeled back the hammers and charged forward, flanking the stampeding herd, bellowing at them with rage and the wild, savage humor that came to him only in moments like this. For the love of killing was upon Will Bentley now, the love of killing and the euphoric triumph of extricating himself from an unwinnable and unjust situation; and now, shouting and laughing, his voice lost in the pounding of hooves and the gunshots and screams of the men still standing in the way of one hundred and fifty charging cattle, he joined the back of the stampede, hurtling forward with the gigantic bovines as they bowled over men and horses and trampled them underfoot.

In among the enemies, Will spotted a raider at the edge, dodging the herd. The man smiled with relief—then his eyes and mouth went wide when he saw Will and the huge bores of the shotgun charging at him.

Will pulled a trigger.

The man's face disappeared in a hail of buckshot.

Will spotted another raider, gave him the second barrel, and hurried to reload the ten-gauge.

But another raider appeared, spotted Will, and started to bring his gun around.

Before Will could respond, Clyde charged forward, slammed into the raider's horse, and bowled over the man and his mount.

The raider scrambled up, gun in hand, and started swinging it toward Will again.

Grabbing the shotgun with his left, Will quick drew the Colt with his right and shot the raider before the man could even line up his sights.

Then Will holstered the Colt, reloaded the messenger gun, and wove amidst the destruction, firing his shotgun; breaking it open, and reloading with deft skill; slashing back and forth and firing again and again, killing a raider every time he pulled a trigger.

When the cattle ran off into the darkness, Will wheeled and

raced back through the destruction. Here and there, dismounted raiders staggered to their feet… only to be blasted into oblivion by a very angry Texan with a shotgun.

The last of them screamed and started running off in the same direction the cattle had gone.

Will ran him down, dropped him with a load of buckshot to the back, and then spotted movement farther out there in the darkness.

A familiar figure atop a big black stallion leapt the creek, fleeing onto Will's family farm.

Sully…

Will charged after him.

CHAPTER 46

Maggie fired the shot that started everything.

The night erupted in gunfire.

Terrified, she fired again.

She heard bullets striking the bunkhouse behind her, felt something tug at her dress, and cried out when something hot sliced across her cheek.

I've been shot, she realized. *Shot in the face!*

Defiantly, she shot at the mass of riders again.

"Maggie!" Will's voice bellowed. "Take cover!"

Her legs obeyed his command though her mind still struggled with the fact that she'd been shot.

Was she dying?

Her face was numb and hot, and her breath came in ragged gasps as she sprinted across the ground, bullets snapping all around her.

Then she was behind a tree close to the house, and her mind

was yanked away again as she heard the gate bang open. The cattle came rushing out in a crazed stampede.

What was happening?

Then she saw Will atop Clyde, saw him toward the back of the herd, driving them forward, directing them toward Teal's men in a rolling wall of muscle and horns.

The stampede bowled over horses. Men, taken utterly by surprise, flew into the air, pinwheeling like tossed dolls and disappearing under the hooves of the charging longhorns.

She longed to fire again but couldn't, not with Will out there in the mix.

Where was he?

Then she caught a glimpse of him in the thick of things, using his shotgun, unseating one raider, then another...

To her left, a raider streaked toward the house with a torch, meaning to set it afire, meaning to burn her home.

She came running out from the tree and fired the Dragoon... and missed.

The man, twenty feet away, jerked his eyes in her direction. He smiled, tossed the flaming stick onto the porch, and pulled a long revolver from his belt.

Maggie fired again, aiming for the breastbone like Will taught her, and that's where the bullet took the raider. He dropped from the saddle and hit hard, and his horse ran off, badly frightened.

Maggie pointed the Dragoon at the crumpled figure of the man, drew back the hammer, and pulled the trigger again, but this time, there was no bang.

The gun was empty!

She thrust a hand into her dress pocket, hunting ammo,

needing to reload, but no... wrong pocket... inside that pocket was the derringer she had been keeping on her ever since Sully's last visit.

She needed ammunition!

Reaching into her other pocket, she found the box and pulled it out with shaking hands and realized she needed to empty the cylinder before loading new cartridges.

Now, how did she do that again? Did she have to pull the tamping lever?

"Don't bother, girl," a man's voice said behind her, startling her badly. "Drop the gun."

She dropped the gun and turned, wishing she'd just retrieved the derringer instead of trying to reload the Dragoon.

But now it was too late, because the man was pointing his gun at her, and if she made a try for the pocket pistol, he'd put a bullet through her heart.

Not that the derringer would do much good at this range anyway. He was twenty yards away. She wouldn't have much of a chance of hitting him at this range with the short-barreled, little weapon.

She moaned, realizing the house had caught fire behind her. The flames spread rapidly, illuminating the darkness around her and warming her with the heat of her burning dream.

Then the man rode slowly into the firelight. He was a small, mean-looking man with a hawklike nose, a graying beard, and dark eyes that shone like chips of polished midnight.

She gasped.

It was Teal.

Maggie reeled. Between Teal and the burning house, it was like she'd been transported back in time to die with her family.

Teal's smile was triumphant. "You're the Dunne girl, the one who got away, the one Sully hired me to kill in the first place, last time I was here."

His words cut her deeply, removing all doubt. She had caused the death of her family by refusing Sully.

"Good luck on my part," Teal said. "I was gonna shoot you when you killed Jerry, but then I saw your hair. You're worth an extra thousand to me alive. Besides, after that stunt your new husband pulled, I might just need you as a hostage before this is all over. The tide seems to have turned."

Her eyes filled with tears.

She wiped them away... and that's when she saw Teal's horse.

Or rather, the horse that Teal was riding. Because that big, beautiful horse could never be Teal's.

It was Father's prize stallion. She loved that horse, and he loved her.

"Bastion," she said.

The magnificent stallion trotted forward, bringing Teal close enough that she could see his scowl when he hauled back on the reins. Then he laughed. "Oh yeah. Guess you would know this horse, wouldn't you? I got him from your old house. Nice payday, that. This stallion's worth more than what was in that bank the Weatherspoons hired me to rob, that's for sure."

"Bastion, sweetie," Maggie said, "it's me, old friend. It's Maggie."

Bastion trotted forward.

Teal, more irritated than ever, hollered at the horse, who ignored him, just as he had ignored Father when Maggie was still a mischievous child and would call the horse to her against Father's will.

"I said whoa," Teal growled as the horse carried him closer, bringing him within ten yards, five...

"Bastion," Maggie said, filling her voice with command. "Kick the sky!"

The powerful stallion responded instantly, rearing up suddenly, surprising Teal, who cursed, nearly falling from the saddle.

Maggie yanked the derringer from her dress and rushed forward.

The horse pounded down, jarring Teal again. He leaned hard, almost slipping from the saddle, and his eyes went wide, seeing her extend her arm.

Teal cursed and tried to bring his gun around, but Maggie was on him then, getting close and angling the gun upward so it wouldn't hurt the horse.

She fired.

Teal screamed and fell hard to the ground with his back to her.

Spewing profanity, he started to rise.

Maggie pushed the two-shot derringer into the back of his skull. "This is for my family," she said, and pulled the trigger one more time.

CHAPTER 47

Will reached the creek and moved forward cautiously, knowing Sully might be holed up here on the old homestead, hoping to spring an ambush.

Everything was deathly still.

Moonlight showed him the tracks of Sully's stallion.

Will took his time following them.

Far behind him, there were two more gunshots.

Even in the darkness, Will could make out every potential hiding spot. The trees, the well, the chicken coop, the house itself.

Inside his former home, candles burned. The muffled voices of a man and woman argued.

Will sat for a moment, scanning the darkness and listening hard.

Sully had probably tucked tail and run for town.

If so, Will would never catch him. Not tonight. Not on Clyde.

Because, while Clyde was hands down the best horse he had ever owned, he could never outrun Sully's thoroughbred stallion.

Back in the direction of his home, there was another gunshot. A few seconds later, another shot followed.

Will listened for several seconds, but there was no more shooting.

The battle seemed to be over.

At least on that side of the creek.

Will eased Clyde forward through the darkness, his eyes flicking from one potential ambush site to another.

He knew them well.

As a young boy, he used them all, grinning as he hid from Daddy, then springing out like a wild Indian, stabbing his father with an imaginary knife.

What fun they had had together, Daddy and him, until a nameless drifter had cut across their property, and Daddy had asked him if he'd like a dipper of water, and the man pulled a revolver and—

The farmhouse door opened behind Will.

He twisted in his seat, bringing the big bores of the ten-gauge to bear not on Sully but the Yankee carpetbagger, Mr. Braintree, who gave a terrified squawk and lifted his hands, rifle and all, high overhead. "Don't shoot!" he begged. "I just wanted to see what all the racket was."

"Hush," Will growled.

And a gunshot shattered the stillness.

The bullet slammed into Will's side, making him grunt.

But he'd seen the muzzle flash. Sully had fired from behind the chicken coop.

Will rushed forward at an angle, putting the coop between him and Sully. Then he stopped Clyde, switched the shotgun to his left hand, and drew his Colt.

He glanced quickly in the direction of the house, making sure Braintree wasn't getting any ideas with that rifle of his.

He wasn't. The carpetbagger had gone back inside and shut the door.

The gunshot hurt bad, but a little prodding told him it had gone in and out of his side, missing his guts, praise God.

"I got you!" Sully's voice cried from behind the coop that Will had built with his own two hands. Everything on this place, either he'd built or his father had. "I saw you flinch. How do you like that, Bentley? Feel good? I'm no coward!"

What an odd thing to declare at a moment like this. Sully's voice had warbled when he'd yelled it, sounding like it might break.

Apparently, it was important to Sully that Will thought he was brave.

What a strange notion. What a strange, twisted man.

"I could've run, but I didn't!" Sully shouted from behind the far corner of the coop. "I stayed, and I shot you, and now, I'm going to kill you. Because I have guts!"

"Maybe you got guts, maybe you don't," Will called back, "but you sure don't have many brains. That coop you're hiding behind? I built it out of scrap wood years ago. I could shoot through it with a decent slingshot."

Will emptied his Colt, blowing holes through the coop.

Sully cried out sharply then fell silent just as abruptly, telling Will he was either dead or hit awful hard.

Will didn't leave it to chance.

He dismounted, walked to the other end of the coop, then blasted the lump on the ground with both barrels.

Whatever Sully had been, he was dead now.

Very, very dead.

Will broke open the messenger gun and loaded two fresh shells and was just about to reload his Colt when, with the rush of battle finally ebbing away, he turned and looked back across the field to where his home burned brightly in the night.

He slammed the empty Colt in its holster, slung the shotgun over one shoulder, ran back to Clyde, climbed aboard, and raced toward home, praying for his friends and family.

CHAPTER 48

"How does it feel, being back in your old room?" Mama asked three days later.

Will shrugged. "Not bad. Though I'd like to provide something nicer for Maggie eventually."

He'd been examining the ceiling, where a new water stain had appeared since he'd last been in his boyhood room... which would now, for a time at least, be his and Maggie's space.

"That's your nature, son. You've always been a good provider. I'm just happy to be home with Pa and the babies. I hope those Yankees never come back."

The battle had been too much for Braintree and his wife. They had abandoned Will's family farm the very next day, leaving with a wagon full of possessions and telling a neighbor on the way out, "That crazy Bentley can have the place for all we care. We're never coming back!"

Will figured he'd head to town at some point and see about

making that official. He'd feel a lot better with a deed to the place. But in the meantime, this would work just fine.

"They won't be back," Will said with a grin. "Too noisy for them here."

For Will, his family, and friends, the battle had gone unbelievably well.

A bullet had grazed Maggie's face and would leave one heck of a scar on her cheek, but it had done no structural damage, and as Will told her over and over, the mark would make her even more gorgeous to him, serving as a reminder of her bravely coming out to fight alongside him then avenging her family against Teal himself.

Will was black-and-blue from his pelvis to partway up his ribcage, but as he had suspected, the bullet wound had not been serious.

None of the others received so much as a scratch.

On Will's side, anyway.

When the dust settled and bodies were counted, nineteen raiders were dead, counting Teal, Sully, Gibbs, and a pair of scoundrels who tried to run south and ended up getting knocked out of their saddles by Will's excellent neighbors, Sam Waters and his boy, Junior.

Will suspected a few more raiders did manage to escape. But that was all right. They had kicked the wrong dog up here, and they weren't liable to come back anytime soon.

Of course, not everything had gone well.

In the wild stampede, several longhorns had been shot dead or wounded badly enough that Will and his friends had put them out of their misery, and another three dozen were still at large despite an effort to gather them.

Worse still, the house had burned along with everything in it, all their food and clothing and furniture and personal items, like Mama's Bible and Rose's journal and Maggie's cameo brooch, which she had borrowed from her mother the night of Teal's first raid, and which had understandably been of great value to her.

The fire also destroyed another thing of great value: Will's saddlebags, which had contained the rest of his hard-earned cash.

The sting of this particular loss was greatly alleviated, however, when they searched the enemy corpses and came away with over a thousand dollars in cash.

They gave a hundred dollars to Sam and Junior Waters, then split the rest of the money equally between those who'd fought: Will, Maggie, Rufus, Jake, Ted, and Farley.

The money would come in handy. In fact, Rufus was in town now with Candy and Rose, loading up the wagon with everything they needed.

They also split the raiders' possessions and horses, except for Bastion and three beautiful thoroughbred mares that had also belonged to Maggie's family.

Maggie was overjoyed to have the horses back, and the horses were clearly happy to be home with her again. They followed her constantly.

Will hoped they would help her get over the terrible battle.

As for him, none of those fine thoroughbreds could hold a candle to his ugly steed.

Clyde had held up under fire like a seasoned warhorse and had even saved Will's life in the heat of battle, slamming into the raider who'd gotten the drop on Will.

Suddenly, Mama gasped. "Soldiers, Will."

Will slung the bandolier across his body and grabbed the ten-gauge. "How many, Mama?"

"Five," she said, leaning close to the window. "Five that I see."

Will relaxed a little. Five was hardly a war party.

"That officer is with them," Mama said.

"Captain Culp," Will said and started for the hallway.

"Wait, son," Mama said. "They're riding up now. Maggie's talking to Captain Culp. She's a good woman, Will. Let her handle this. We can listen through the window."

From Will's angle beside the window, he could not only hear but also see Culp and Maggie as they exchanged pleasantries.

"You want us to search the house for Bentley?" the big sergeant who'd tried to bait Will into a fight asked Culp.

"No, Sergeant Garrity, that won't be necessary. I'm certain Miss Dunne would tell us if he was inside. Take the other men out to the perimeters and stand watch in case he tries to come back."

Garrity hurried off.

Turning to Maggie, Captain Culp said, "I was pleased to hear that Mr. Bentley had fled the region, Miss Dunne."

He spoke loudly, as if he wanted others to hear his message. Folks listening from beside the window, for example.

"Yes," Captain Culp said, "I'm very pleased that he's gone off because he's a renegade now. My superiors in the North want me to apprehend him."

"Thank you for telling me, sir," Maggie said.

Culp gave her a little bow. "This is not my doing, of course, ma'am. The way I see it, he has done the Union a service, ridding us of Teal and, if I'm honest, Sully Weatherspoon. But I am a soldier, ma'am, and I will do my duty."

"I don't think that would surprise Mr. Bentley," Maggie said. "He spoke very highly of you, sir."

"Thank you, ma'am. That is a pleasure to hear. I have never sought the approval of others, but a man like Will Bentley, well, having his respect would mean something to me."

"You have it, sir. I assure you of that."

Culp gave another bow. "If Mr. Bentley were here, I would tell him to lie low until this all blows over. I would even suggest that he leave home for a while. It's a shame he doesn't have someplace to go. A cattle drive, perhaps, something like that."

Will could all but hear Culp wink. He was a good man, the captain, a very good man, even if he did wear the blue. He was exactly the sort of fellow the Union needed to send if they really hoped to set things right in Texas again.

"By the time he returned from a trip like that," Culp continued, "I might be able to sort things out here. It might take weeks or possibly even months for me to do that, but I think I will be able to make this trouble go away. Until then, I do hope our paths will not cross again, because I believe Will Bentley is a good man, and once this is all over, I would be honored to count him among my friends."

"Yes, Captain Culp," Maggie said. "Will Bentley is the best man I've ever known. And I am certain he would be honored to call you his friend."

That's the truth, Will thought, watching the bluebelly captain ride off to gather his men.

Culp had warned him and bought him some time, and Will believed that the captain would do his best to clear Will's name.

Will was grateful.

Yes, he would have to go away for a while, but things were in a good state here now—or would be, once Rufus returned with the supplies.

Will wasn't sure what he would do next. Maybe drive cattle up the Chisholm Trail.

Or maybe Maggie, Mama, and Rose would want to go somewhere with him.

So long as he was with them, he'd be the happiest man in Texas.

Whatever the case, he wasn't worried. But then again, he'd never put much stock in worrying, and he wasn't about to now.

#

THANK YOU FOR READING *THE PROVIDER*.

The adventures of Will and Maggie continue in *The Provider 2*.

If you enjoyed this story, please be a friend and leave a review. When you leave even a short review, you just bought my family dinner, because Amazon will show the book to more people. I sure would appreciate your help.

If you enjoyed the book but don't have time to review, please consider leaving a 5-star rating. It's quick and simple and helps me get this new series off the ground.

I love Westerns and hope to bring you 8 or 10 a year. To hear about new releases, special sales, and giveaways, [join my reader list](#).

Once more, thanks for reading. I hope our paths cross again.

Until then, don't approach a bull from the front, a horse from the rear, or a fool from any direction.

John

ABOUT THE AUTHOR

I was born six months before man landed on the moon and lucky enough to grow up in the country, where my family lived largely off the land.

When I wasn't fishing, exploring the woods, or weeding the garden, I devoured comic books like *Two-Gun Kid* and *The Rawhide Kid* before moving on to the exciting adventure stories of Jack London and Louis L'Amour.

Our black-and-white TV only got three channels, though you could lose one and pick up another if you went outside and messed with the antenna. On its grainy screen, we watched *Gunsmoke*, *Bonanza*, and movies starring John Wayne and Clint Eastwood.

Now a husband and father, I love traveling the West and reading history and fiction alike. My favorite authors are Louis L'Amour, Elmore Leonard, C.J. Petit, and R.O. Lane.

ALSO BY JOHN DEACON

John's Amazon author page has all of his books in various formats: Kindle, paperback, hardcover, and audiobook.

A Man Called Justice (Silent Justice #1)

Justice Returns (Silent Justice #2)

Final Justice (Silent Justice #3)

Justice Rides Again (Silent Justice #4)

Destitution

Heck's Journey (Heck & Hope #1)

Heck's Valley (Heck & Hope #2)

Heck's Gold (Heck & Hope #3)

Heck's Gamble (Heck & Hope #4)

Heck's Stand (Heck & Hope #5)

Lobo (The Lobo Trilogy #1)

Lobo 2 (The Lobo Trilogy #2)

Lobo 3 (The Lobo Trilogy #3)

The Provider (The Provider Saga #1)

The Provider 2 (The Provider Saga #2)

The Provider 3 (The Provider Saga #3)

The Provider 4 (The Provider Saga #4)

Kip (Kip Callahan #1)

Printed in Great Britain
by Amazon